#1
ON the CASE with
HOLMES and WATSON

SHERLOCK HOLMES

and a Scandal in Bohemia

Based on the stories of
Sir Arthur Conan Doyle

Adapted by **Murray Shaw** and **M. J. Cosson**
Illustrated by **Sophie Rohrbach**

GRAPHIC UNIVERSE™ · MINNEAPOLIS · NEW YORK · LONDON

Grateful acknowledgment to Dame Jean Conan Doyle for permission to use the Sherlock Holmes characters created by Sir Arthur Conan Doyle

Graphic Universe™
A division of Lerner Publishing Group, Inc.
241 First Avenue North
Minneapolis, MN 55401 U.S.A.

Website address: www.lernerbooks.com

Library of Congress Cataloging-in-Publication Data

Shaw, Murray.
    #1 Sherlock Holmes and a scandal in Bohemia / adapted by Murray Shaw and M.J. Cosson ; illustrated by Sophie Rohrbach ; from the original stories by Sir Arthur Conan Doyle.
        p.   cm. — (On the case with Holmes and Watson)
    Summary: Retold in graphic novel form, Sherlock Holmes attempts to retrieve a photograph being used to blackmail the King of Bohemia and finds something even more valuable. Includes a section explaining Holmes's reasoning and the clues he used to solve the mystery.
        ISBN 978-0-7613-6185-5 (lib. bdg. : alk. paper)
        1. Graphic novels. (1. Graphic novels. 2. Doyle, Arthur Conan, Sir, 1859–1930. Scandal in Bohemia—Adaptations. 3. Mystery and detective stories.)
    I. Cosson, M. J. II. Rohrbach, Sophie, ill. III. Doyle, Arthur Conan, Sir, 1859–1930. Scandal in Bohemia. IV. Title. V. Title: Scandal in Bohemia.
    PZ7.7.S46She 2011
    741.5'973—dc22   2009051763

Manufactured in the United States of America
1—CG—7/15/10

The Story of
SHERLOCK HOLMES
The Famous Detective

Sherlock Holmes and his helpful friend Dr. John Watson are fictional characters created by British writer Sir Arthur Conan Doyle. Doyle published his first novel about the pair, *A Study in Scarlet*, in 1887, and it became very successful. Doyle went on to write fifty-six short stories, as well as three more novels about Holmes's adventures—*The Sign of Four* (1890), *The Hound of the Baskervilles* (1902), and *The Valley of Fear* (1915).

Sherlock Holmes and Dr. Watson have become some of the most famous book characters of all time. Holmes spent most of his time solving mysteries, but he also had a wide array of hobbies, such as playing the violin, boxing, and sword fighting. Watson, a retired army doctor, met Holmes through a mutual friend when Holmes was looking for a roommate. Watson lived with Holmes for several years at 221B Baker Street before marrying and moving out. However, after his marriage, Watson continued to assist Holmes with his cases.

The original versions of the Sherlock Holmes stories are still printed, and many have been made into movies and television shows. Readers continue to be impressed by Holmes's detective methods of observation and scientific reason.

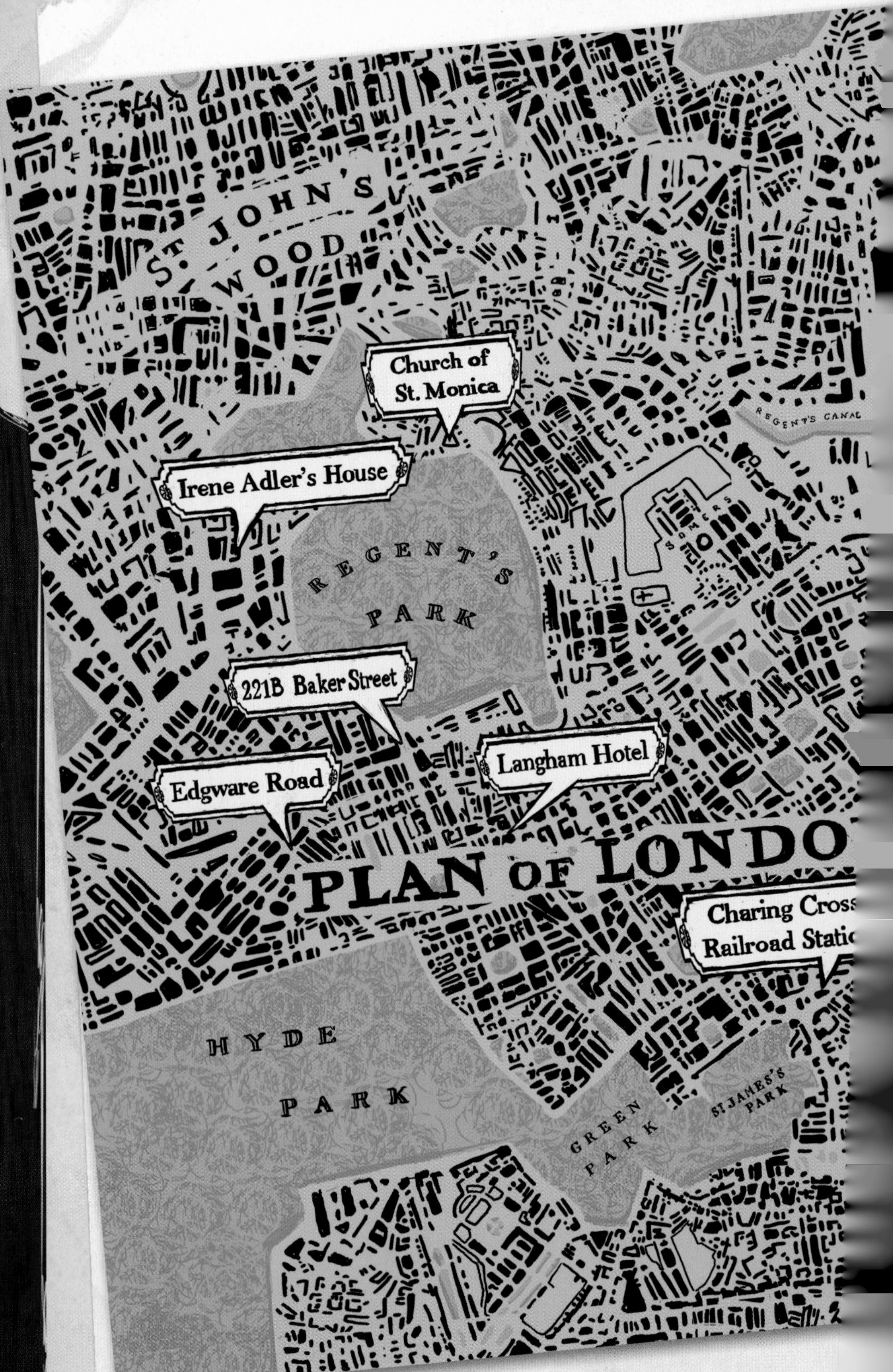
St. John's Wood
Church of St. Monica
Regent's Canal
Irene Adler's House
Regent's Park
Somers
221B Baker Street
Langham Hotel
Edgware Road
Plan of Londo
Charing Cross Railroad Static
Hyde Park
Green Park
St. James's Park

CHARACTER LIST

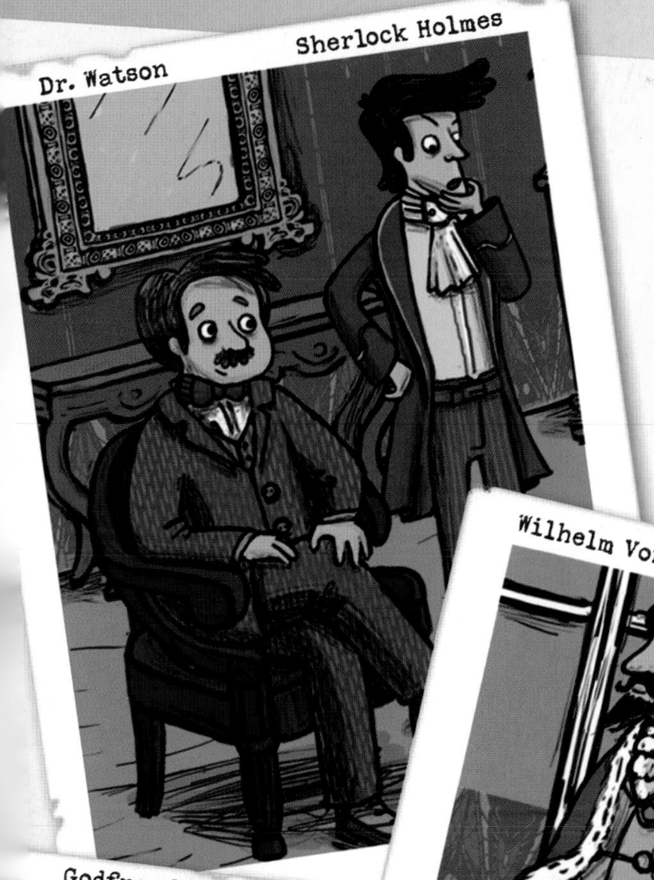
Dr. Watson
Sherlock Holmes

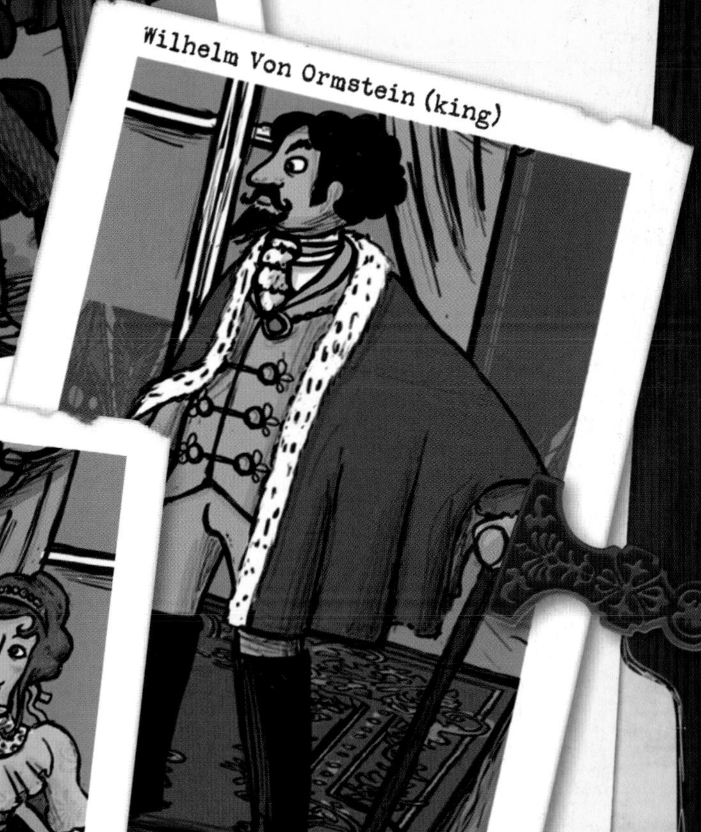
Wilhelm Von Ormstein (king)

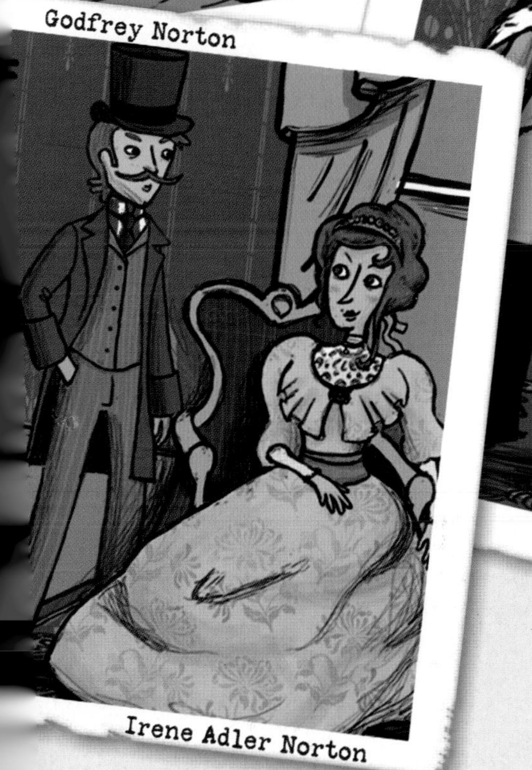
Godfrey Norton
Irene Adler Norton

From the Desk of
John H. Watson, M.D.

My name is Dr. John H. Watson. For several years, I have been assisting my friend, Sherlock Holmes, in solving mysteries throughout the bustling city of London and beyond. Holmes is a peculiar man—always questioning and reasoning his way through various problems. But when I first met him in 1878, I was immediately intrigued by his oddities.

Holmes has always been more daring than I, and his logical deduction never ceases to amaze me. I have begun writing down all of the adventures I have with Holmes. This is one of those stories.

Sincerely,

Dr. Watson

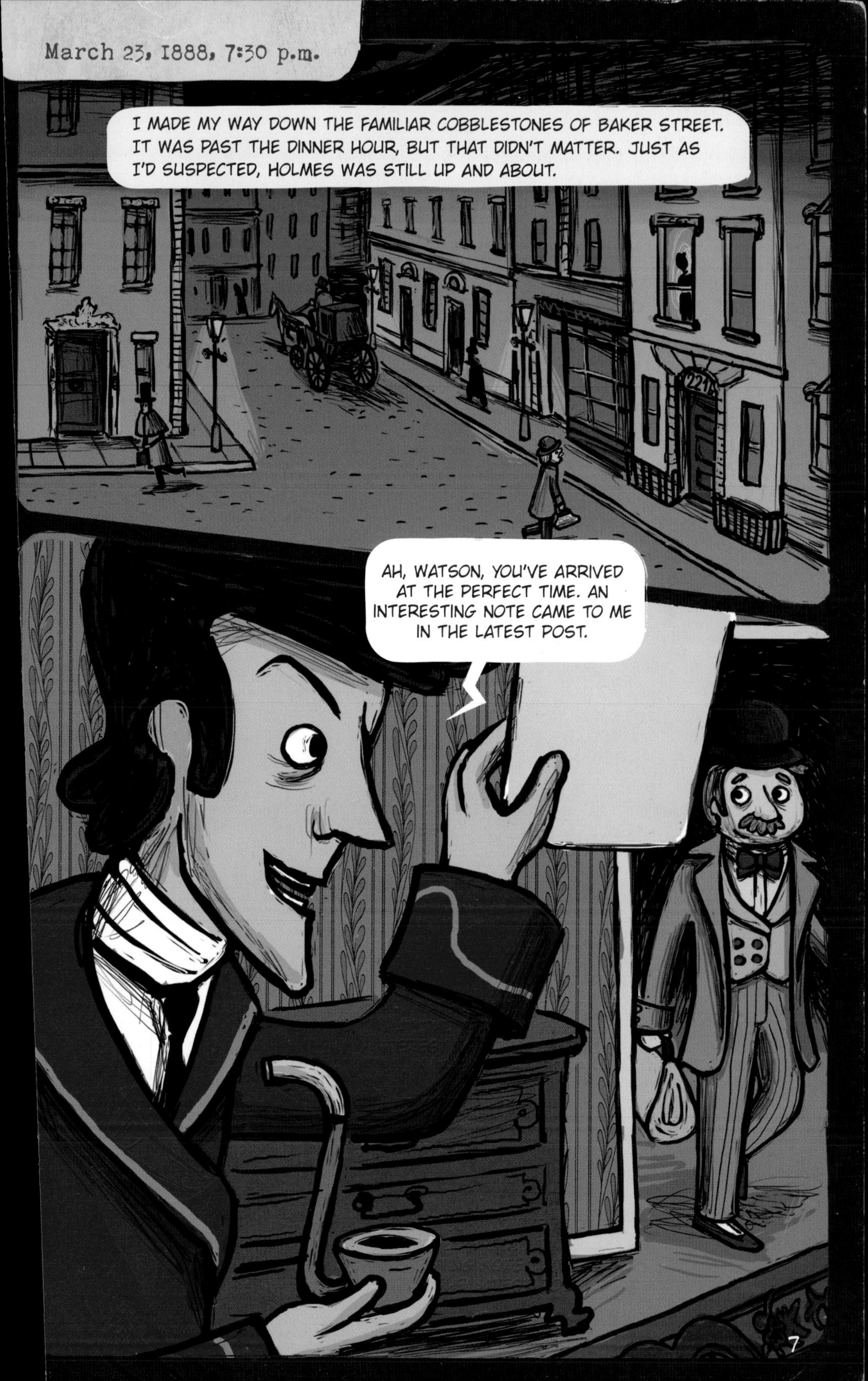
March 23, 1888, 7:30 p.m.
I MADE MY WAY DOWN THE FAMILIAR COBBLESTONES OF BAKER STREET. IT WAS PAST THE DINNER HOUR, BUT THAT DIDN'T MATTER. JUST AS I'D SUSPECTED, HOLMES WAS STILL UP AND ABOUT.
221
AH, WATSON, YOU'VE ARRIVED AT THE PERFECT TIME. AN INTERESTING NOTE CAME TO ME IN THE LATEST POST.

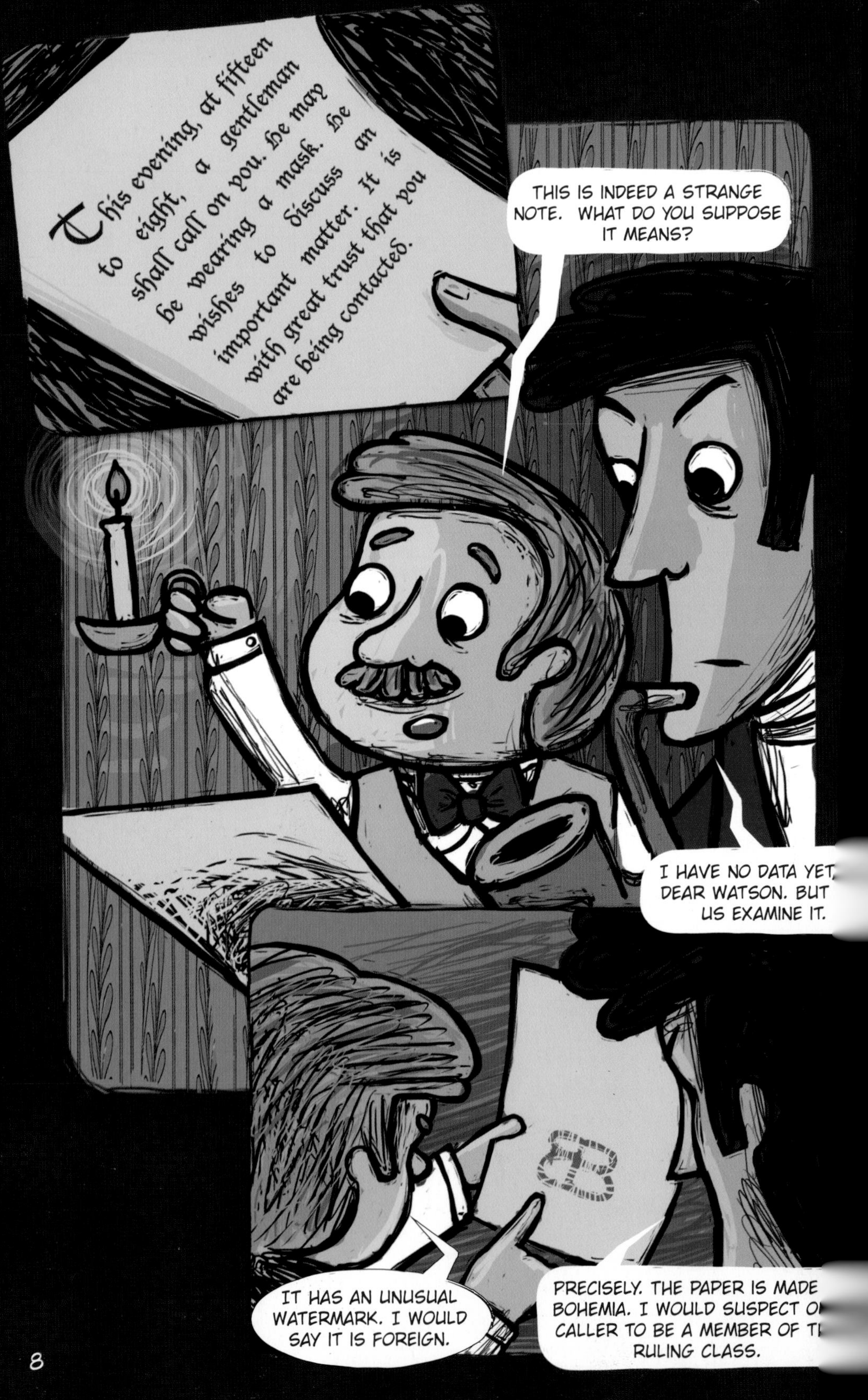
This evening, at fifteen to eight, a gentleman shall call on you. He may be wearing a mask. He wishes to discuss an important matter. It is with great trust that you are being contacted.
THIS IS INDEED A STRANGE NOTE. WHAT DO YOU SUPPOSE IT MEANS?
I HAVE NO DATA YET, DEAR WATSON. BUT US EXAMINE IT.
IT HAS AN UNUSUAL WATERMARK. I WOULD SAY IT IS FOREIGN.
PRECISELY. THE PAPER IS MADE BOHEMIA. I WOULD SUSPECT O CALLER TO BE A MEMBER OF T RULING CLASS.

As he spoke, we both heard the sound of horse's hooves and carriage wheels outside. We went to the window and looked down to see an ornate carriage and two handsome horses waiting at the curb below. There would be money in this case! A moment later, there was a knock on the door.

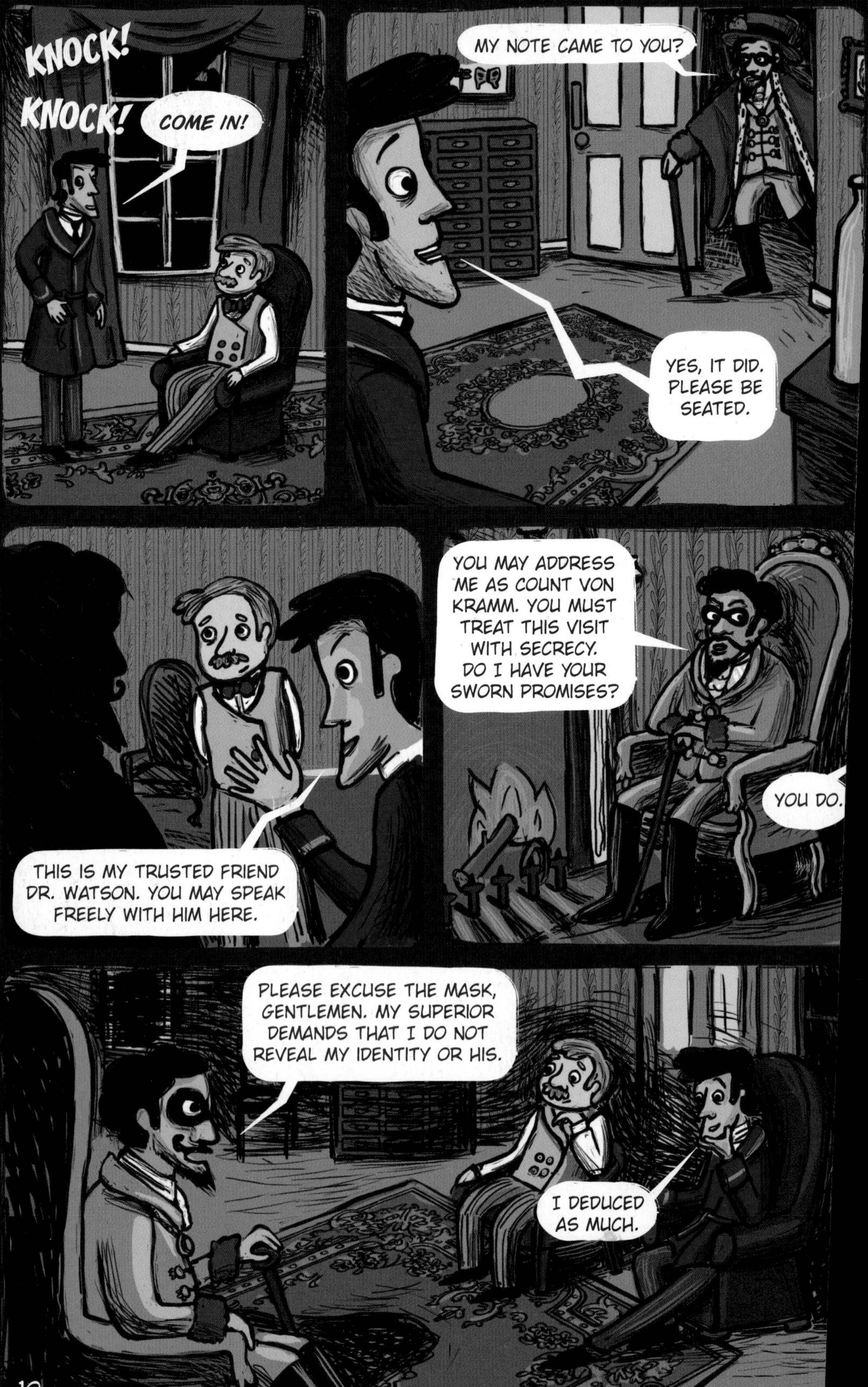
KNOCK!
KNOCK!
COME IN!
MY NOTE CAME TO YOU?
YES, IT DID. PLEASE BE SEATED.
THIS IS MY TRUSTED FRIEND DR. WATSON. YOU MAY SPEAK FREELY WITH HIM HERE.
YOU MAY ADDRESS ME AS COUNT VON KRAMM. YOU MUST TREAT THIS VISIT WITH SECRECY. DO I HAVE YOUR SWORN PROMISES?
YOU DO.
PLEASE EXCUSE THE MASK, GENTLEMEN. MY SUPERIOR DEMANDS THAT I DO NOT REVEAL MY IDENTITY OR HIS.
I DEDUCED AS MUCH.

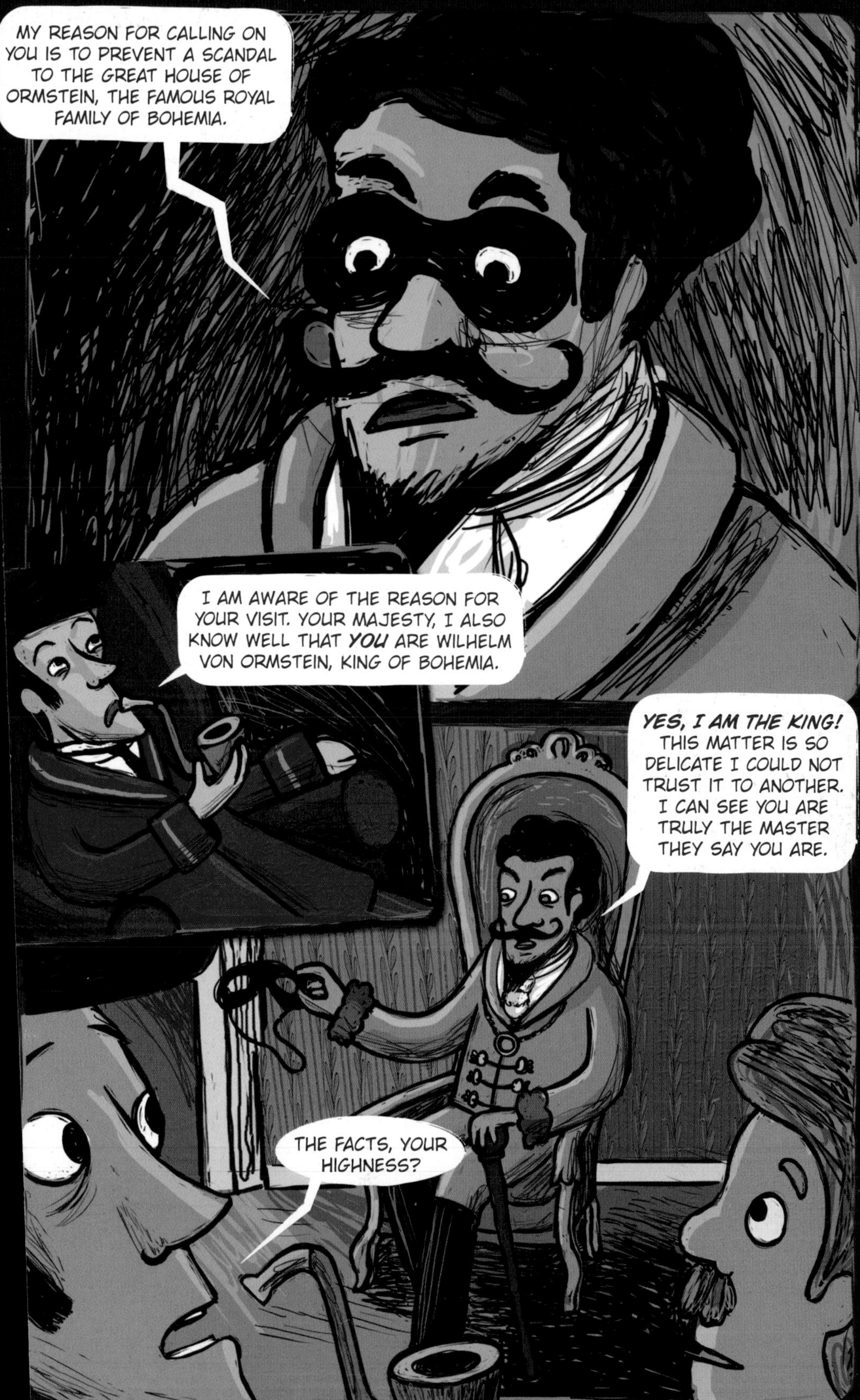
MY REASON FOR CALLING ON YOU IS TO PREVENT A SCANDAL TO THE GREAT HOUSE OF ORMSTEIN, THE FAMOUS ROYAL FAMILY OF BOHEMIA.
I AM AWARE OF THE REASON FOR YOUR VISIT. YOUR MAJESTY, I ALSO KNOW WELL THAT *YOU* ARE WILHELM VON ORMSTEIN, KING OF BOHEMIA.
YES, I AM THE KING! THIS MATTER IS SO DELICATE I COULD NOT TRUST IT TO ANOTHER. I CAN SEE YOU ARE TRULY THE MASTER THEY SAY YOU ARE.
THE FACTS, YOUR HIGHNESS?

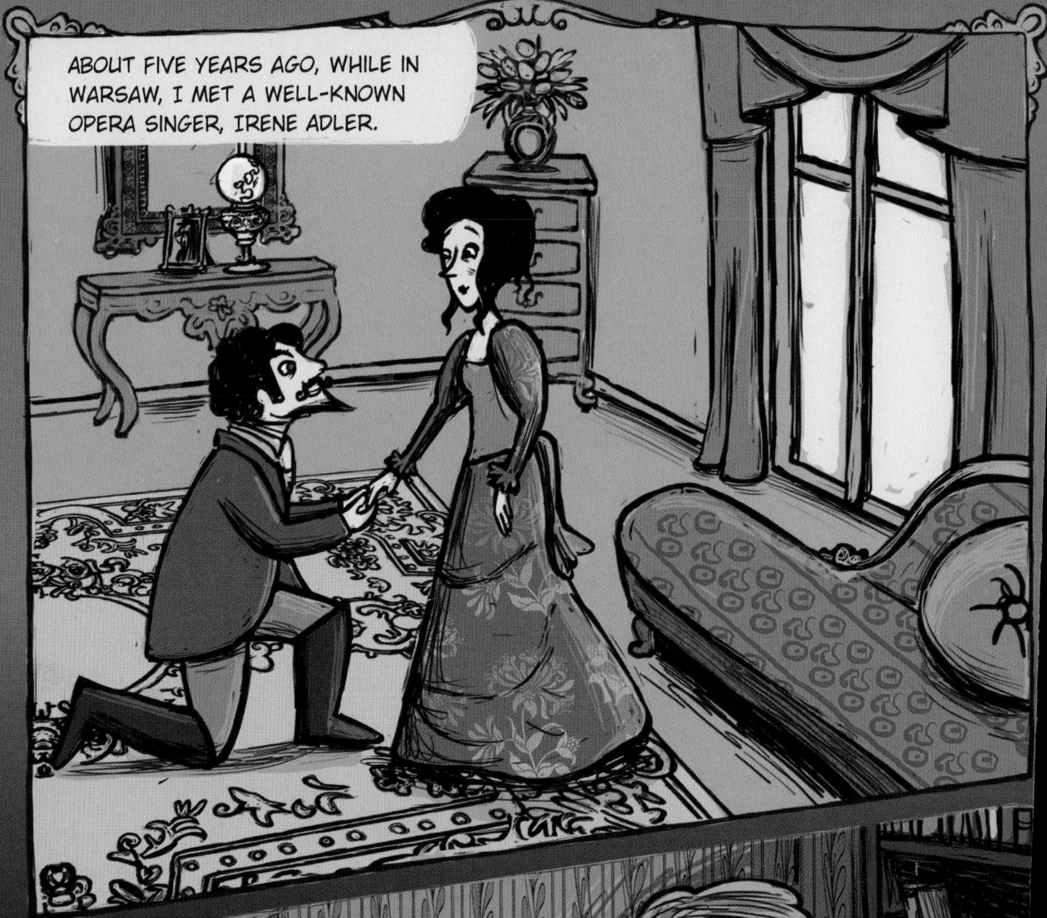
ABOUT FIVE YEARS AGO, WHILE IN WARSAW, I MET A WELL-KNOWN OPERA SINGER, IRENE ADLER.

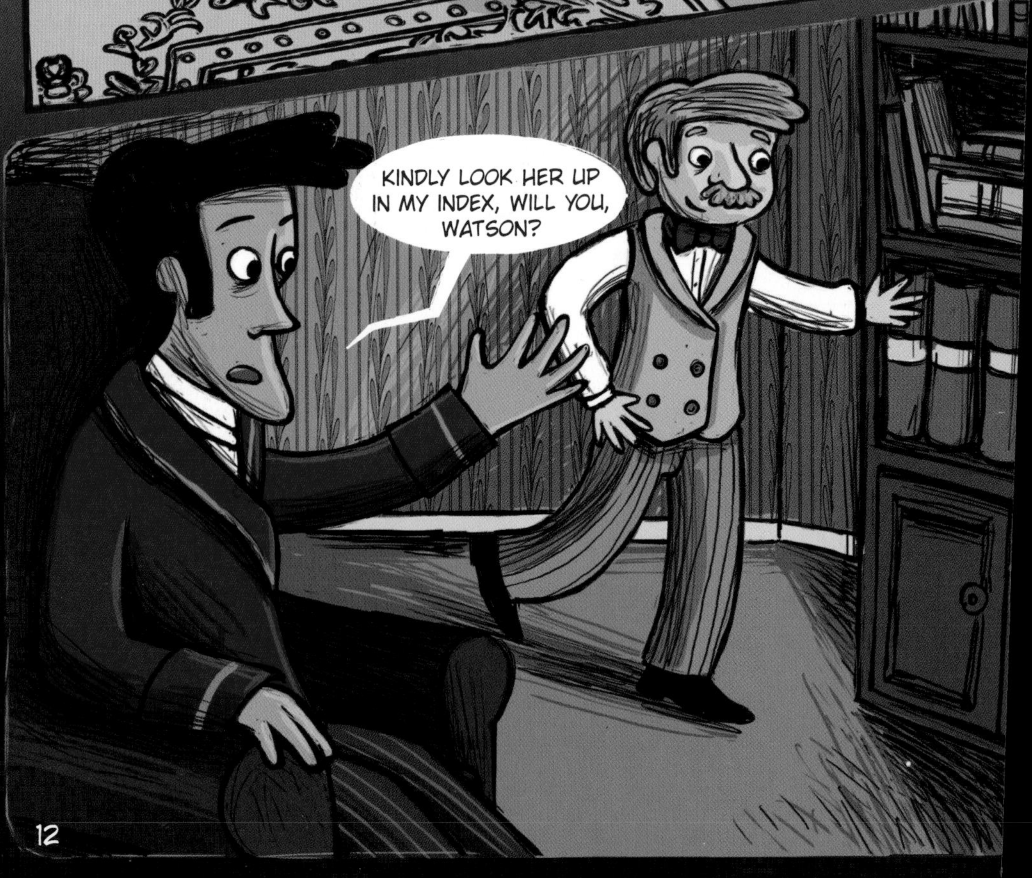
KINDLY LOOK HER UP IN MY INDEX, WILL YOU, WATSON?

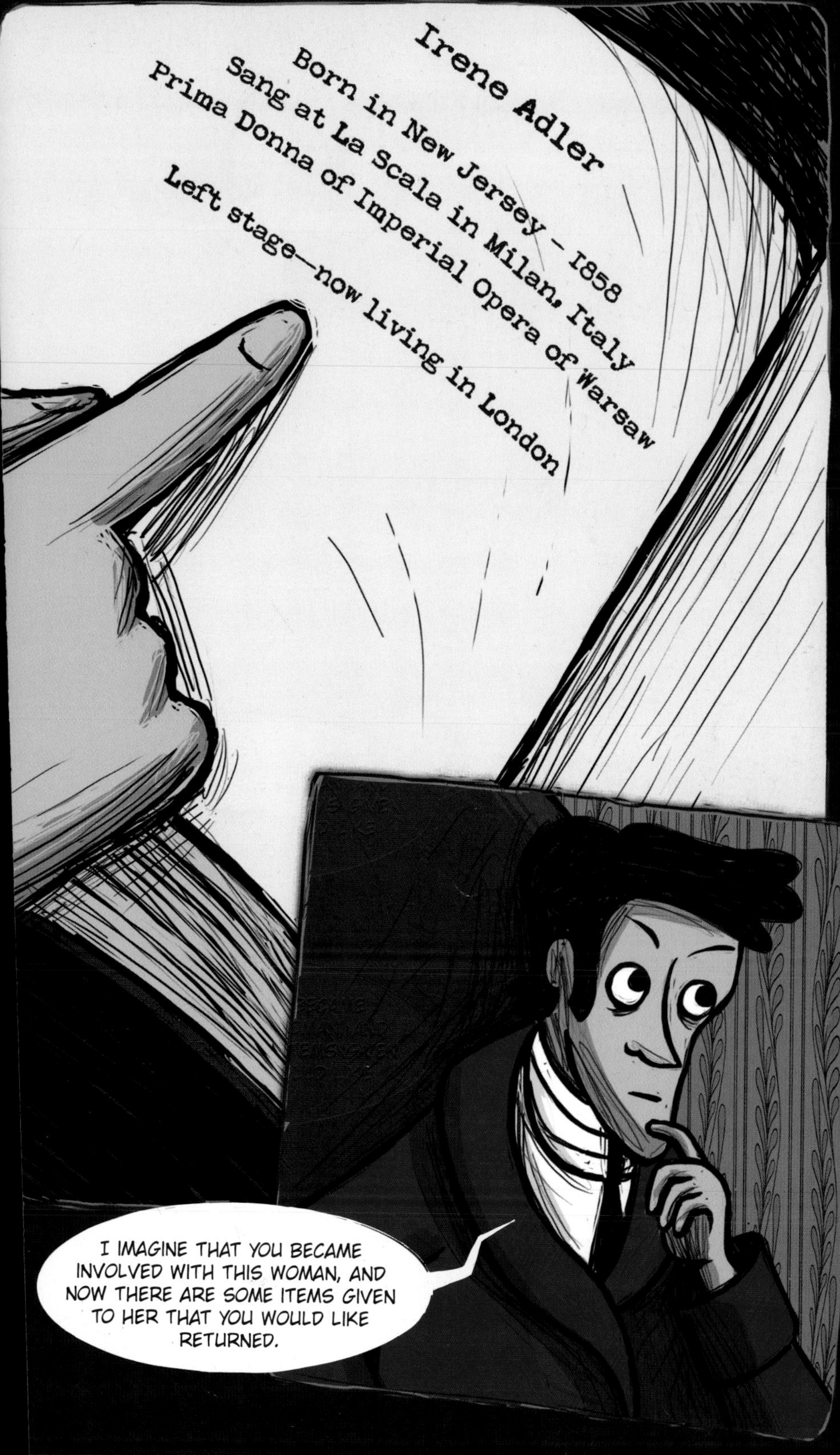
Irene Adler
Born in New Jersey - 1858
Sang at La Scala in Milan, Italy
Prima Donna of Imperial Opera of Warsaw
Left stage—now living in London
I IMAGINE THAT YOU BECAME INVOLVED WITH THIS WOMAN, AND NOW THERE ARE SOME ITEMS GIVEN TO HER THAT YOU WOULD LIKE RETURNED.

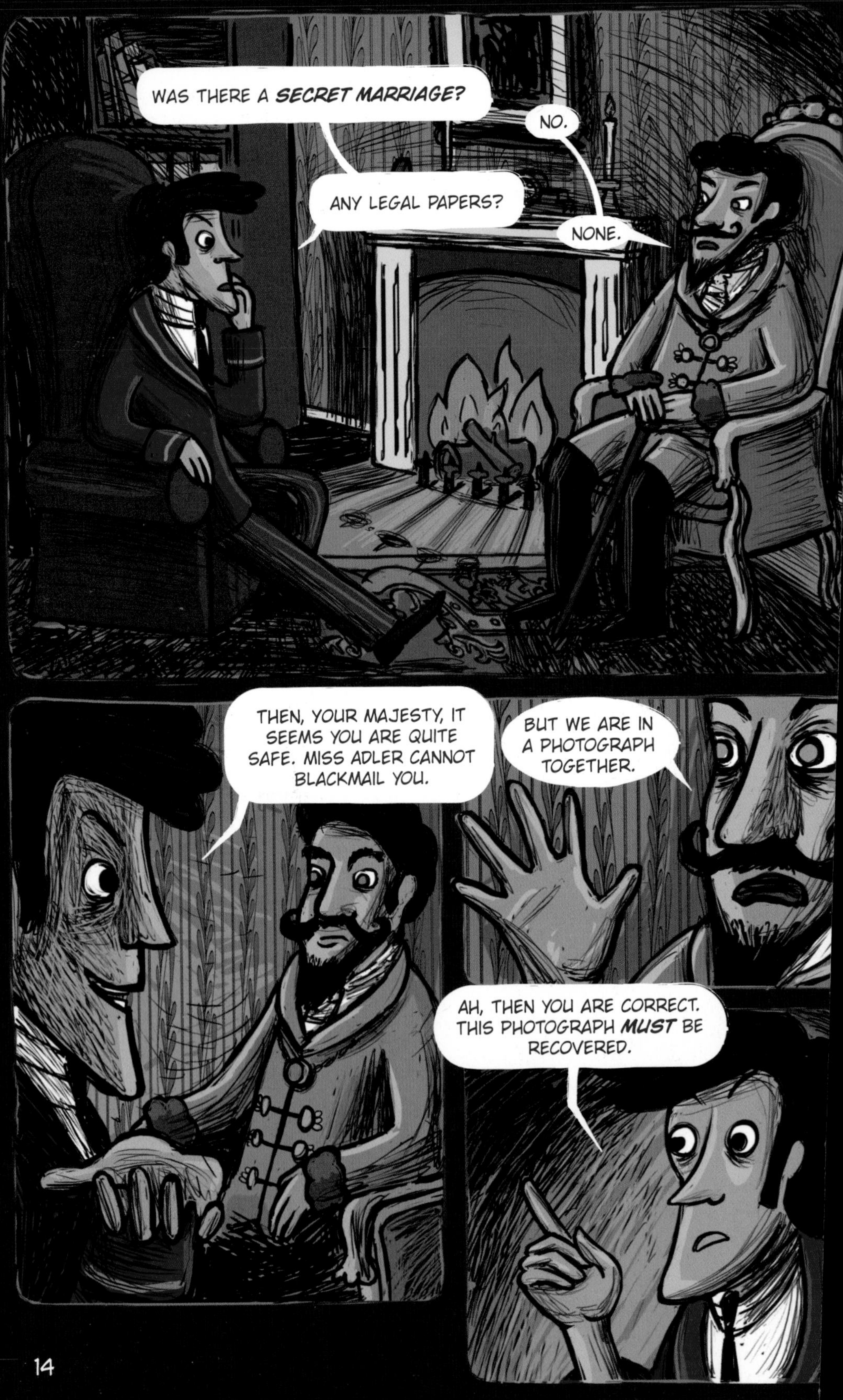
WAS THERE A SECRET MARRIAGE?
NO.
ANY LEGAL PAPERS?
NONE.
THEN, YOUR MAJESTY, IT SEEMS YOU ARE QUITE SAFE. MISS ADLER CANNOT BLACKMAIL YOU.
BUT WE ARE IN A PHOTOGRAPH TOGETHER.
AH, THEN YOU ARE CORRECT. THIS PHOTOGRAPH MUST BE RECOVERED.

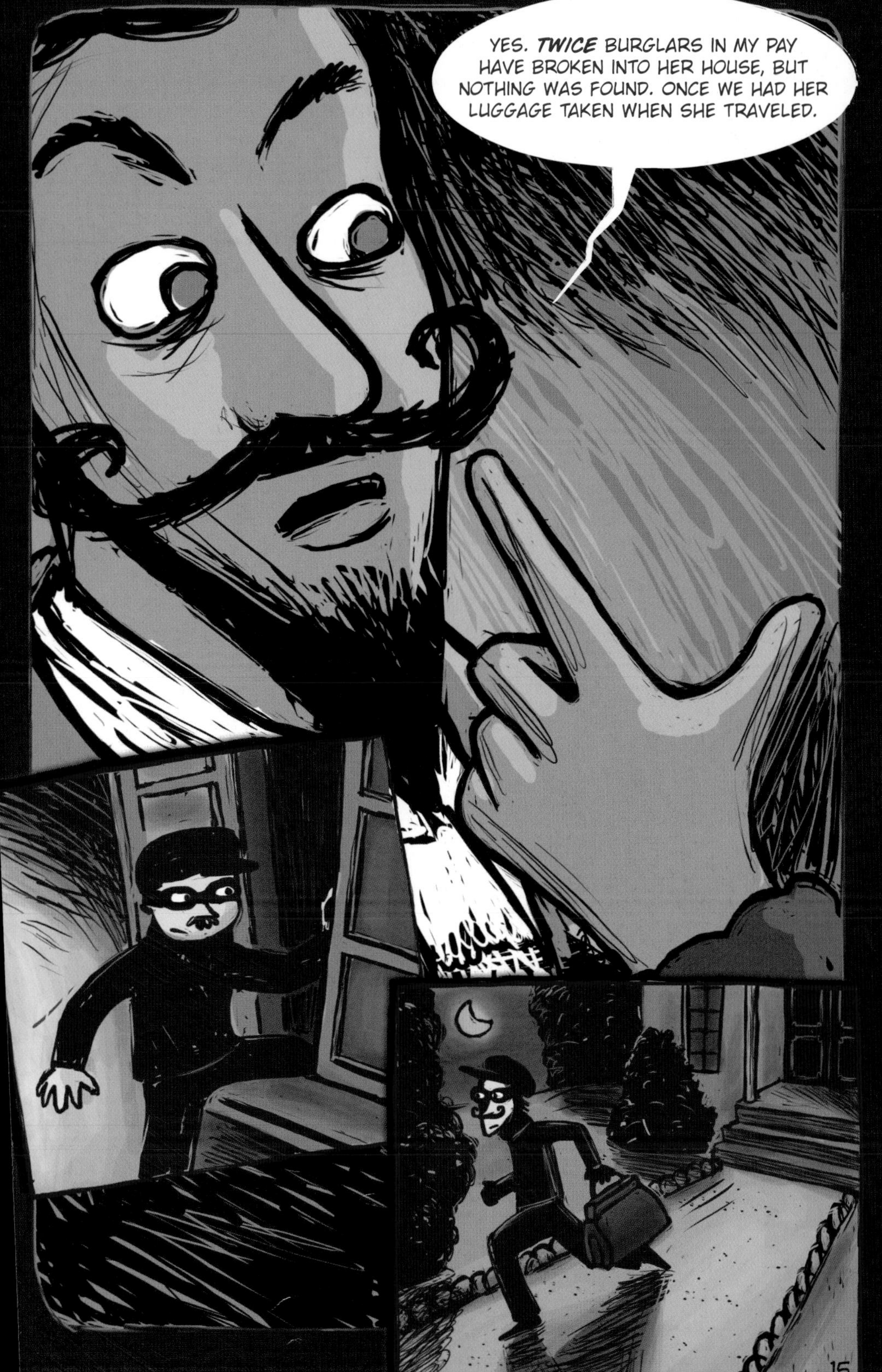
YES. *TWICE* BURGLARS IN MY PAY HAVE BROKEN INTO HER HOUSE, BUT NOTHING WAS FOUND. ONCE WE HAD HER LUGGAGE TAKEN WHEN SHE TRAVELED.

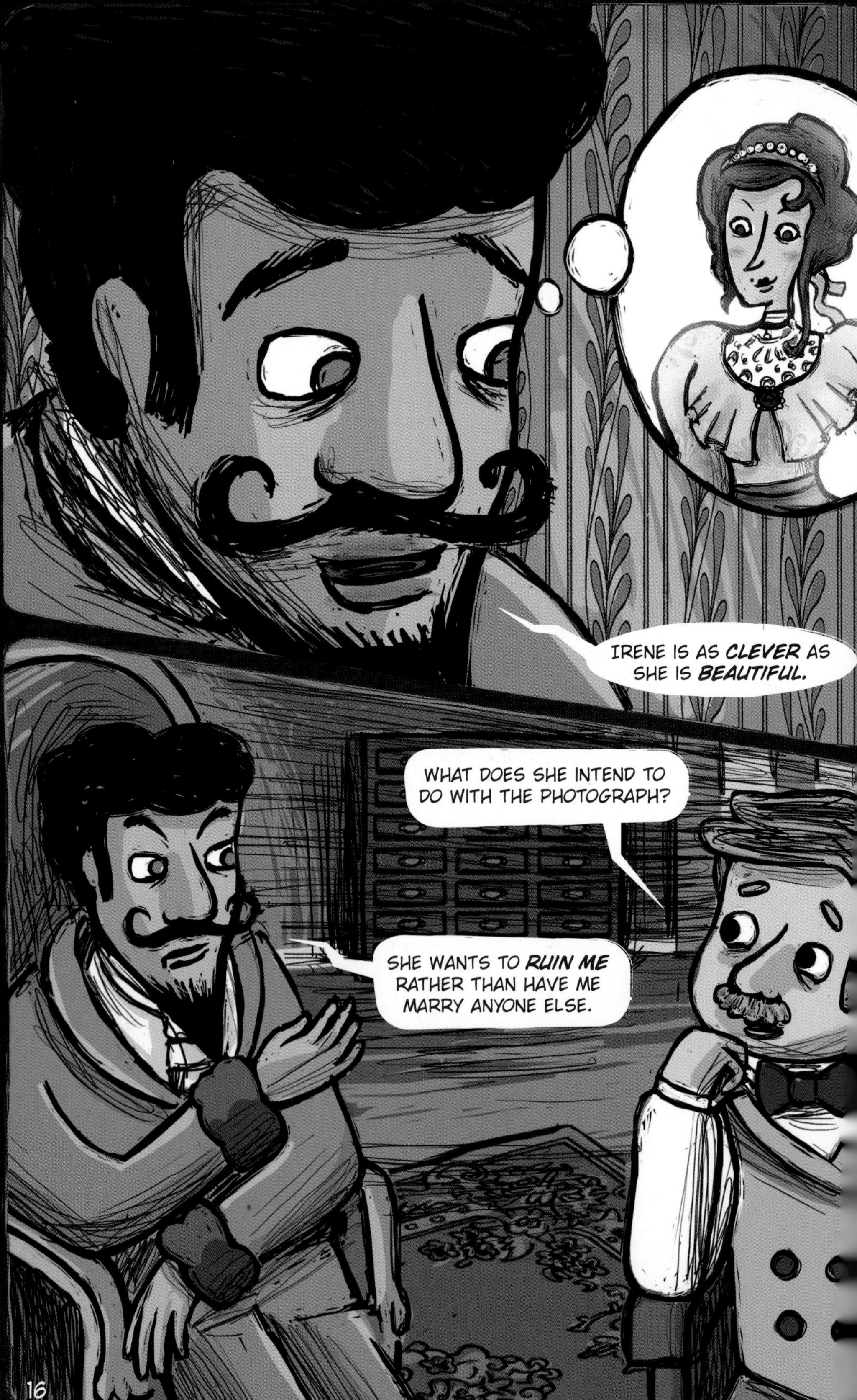
IRENE IS AS **CLEVER** AS SHE IS **BEAUTIFUL.**
WHAT DOES SHE INTEND TO DO WITH THE PHOTOGRAPH?
SHE WANTS TO **RUIN ME** RATHER THAN HAVE ME MARRY ANYONE ELSE.

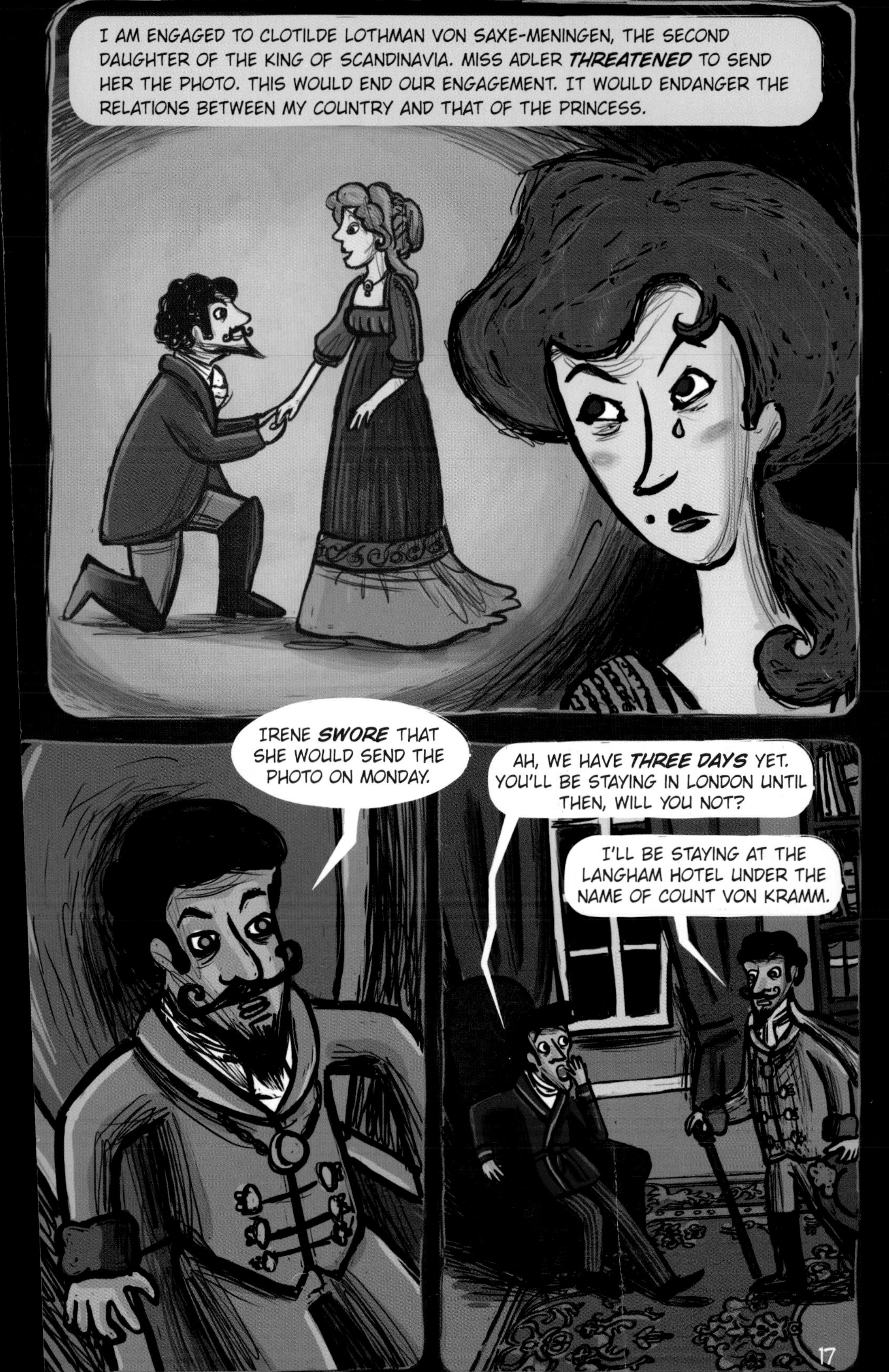
I AM ENGAGED TO CLOTILDE LOTHMAN VON SAXE-MENINGEN, THE SECOND DAUGHTER OF THE KING OF SCANDINAVIA. MISS ADLER ***THREATENED*** TO SEND HER THE PHOTO. THIS WOULD END OUR ENGAGEMENT. IT WOULD ENDANGER THE RELATIONS BETWEEN MY COUNTRY AND THAT OF THE PRINCESS.
IRENE ***SWORE*** THAT SHE WOULD SEND THE PHOTO ON MONDAY.
AH, WE HAVE ***THREE DAYS*** YET. YOU'LL BE STAYING IN LONDON UNTIL THEN, WILL YOU NOT?
I'LL BE STAYING AT THE LANGHAM HOTEL UNDER THE NAME OF COUNT VON KRAMM.

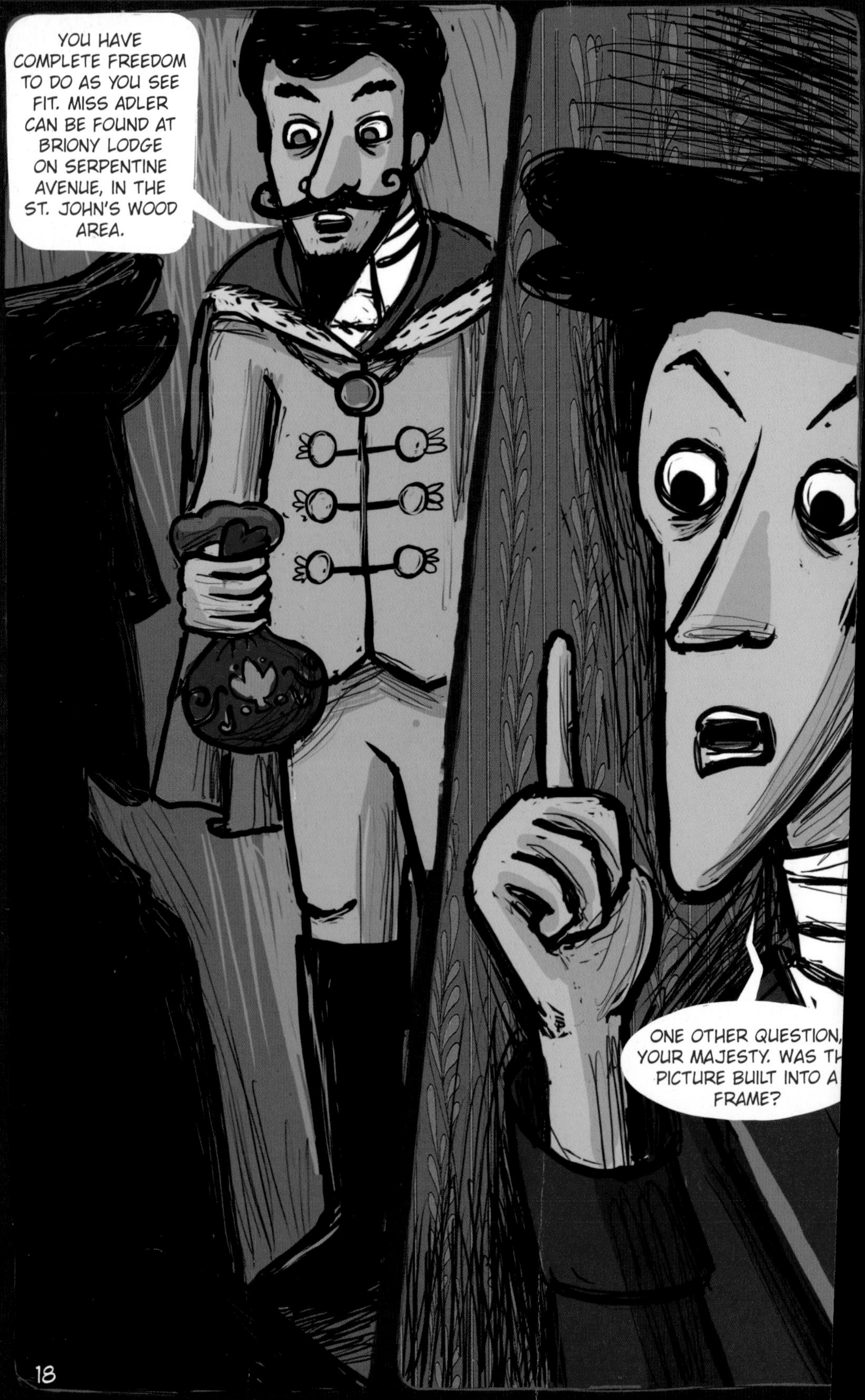
YOU HAVE COMPLETE FREEDOM TO DO AS YOU SEE FIT. MISS ADLER CAN BE FOUND AT BRIONY LODGE ON SERPENTINE AVENUE, IN THE ST. JOHN'S WOOD AREA.
ONE OTHER QUESTION, YOUR MAJESTY. WAS TH PICTURE BUILT INTO A FRAME?

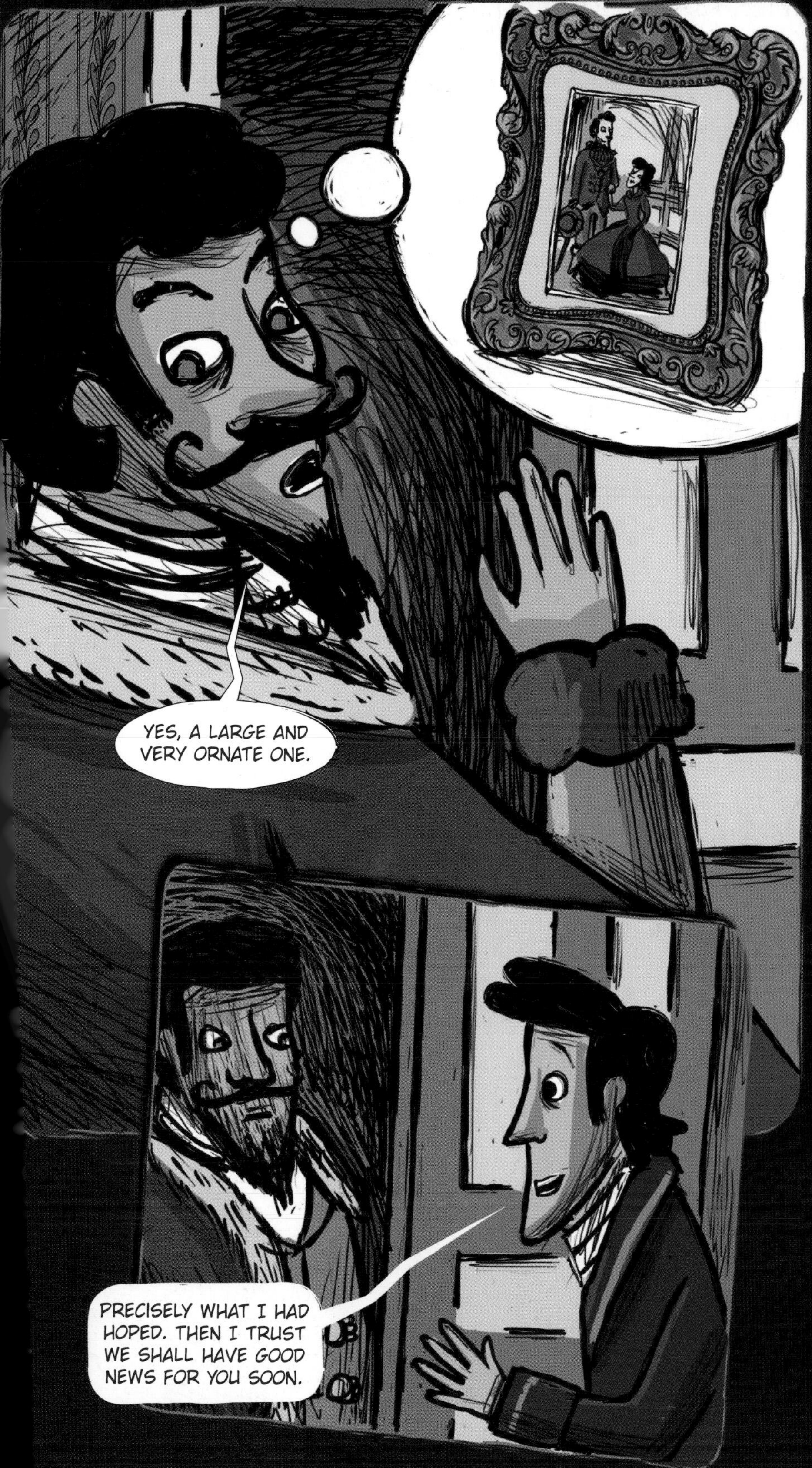
YES, A LARGE AND VERY ORNATE ONE.
PRECISELY WHAT I HAD HOPED. THEN I TRUST WE SHALL HAVE GOOD NEWS FOR YOU SOON.

March 24, 1888, 3:00 p.m.

Holmes requested my assistance for this unusual case. Of course, I agreed to help, excited at the prospect of yet another adventure with him. Holmes asked me to return to his apartment the next day at three o'clock.

I returned to the Baker Street lodging promptly at three, but Holmes was not there. Unsure of his whereabouts, I decided to wait. At about four o'clock, I heard someone stumbling on the steps.

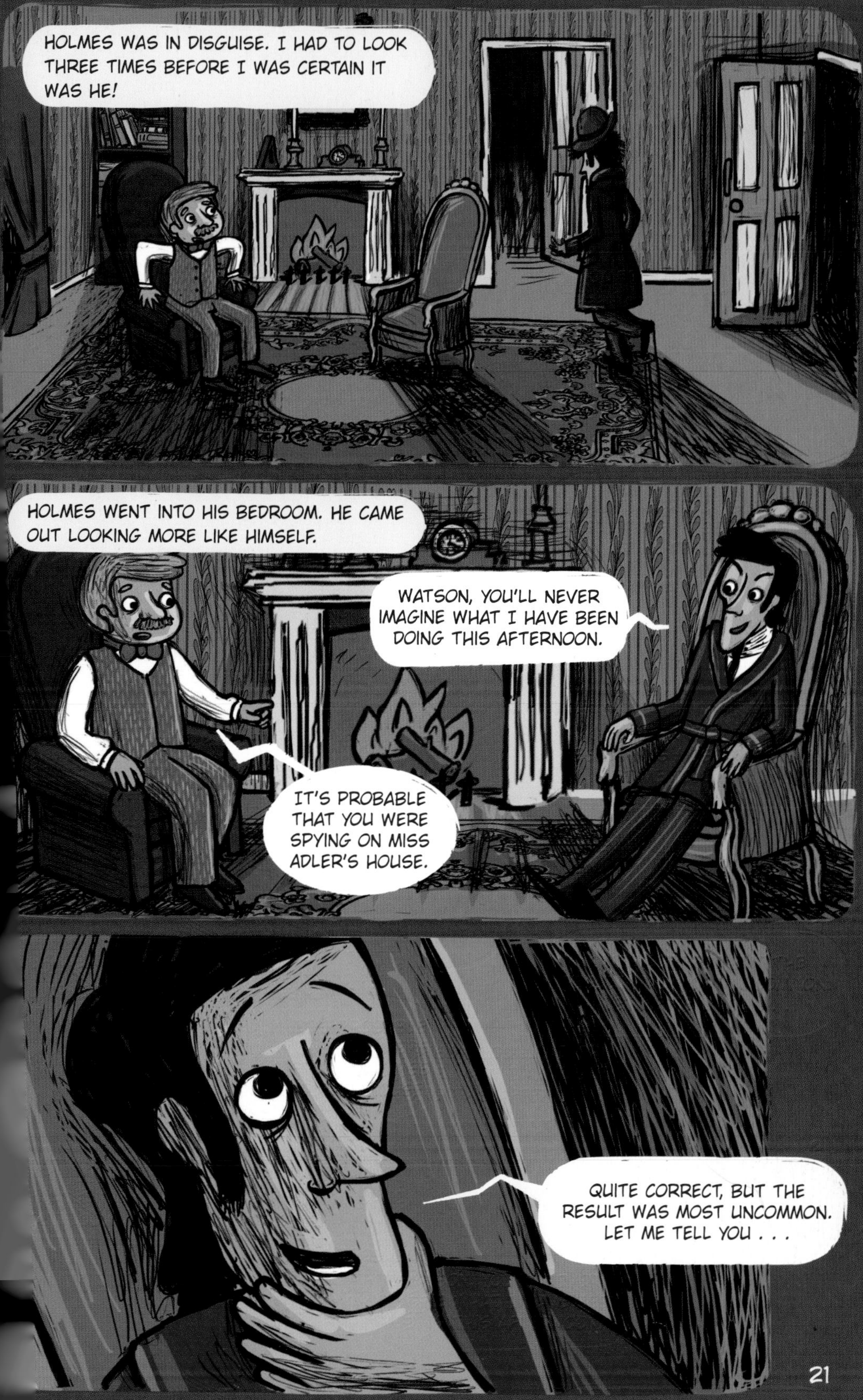
HOLMES WAS IN DISGUISE. I HAD TO LOOK THREE TIMES BEFORE I WAS CERTAIN IT WAS HE!
HOLMES WENT INTO HIS BEDROOM. HE CAME OUT LOOKING MORE LIKE HIMSELF.
WATSON, YOU'LL NEVER IMAGINE WHAT I HAVE BEEN DOING THIS AFTERNOON.
IT'S PROBABLE THAT YOU WERE SPYING ON MISS ADLER'S HOUSE.
QUITE CORRECT, BUT THE RESULT WAS MOST UNCOMMON. LET ME TELL YOU . . .

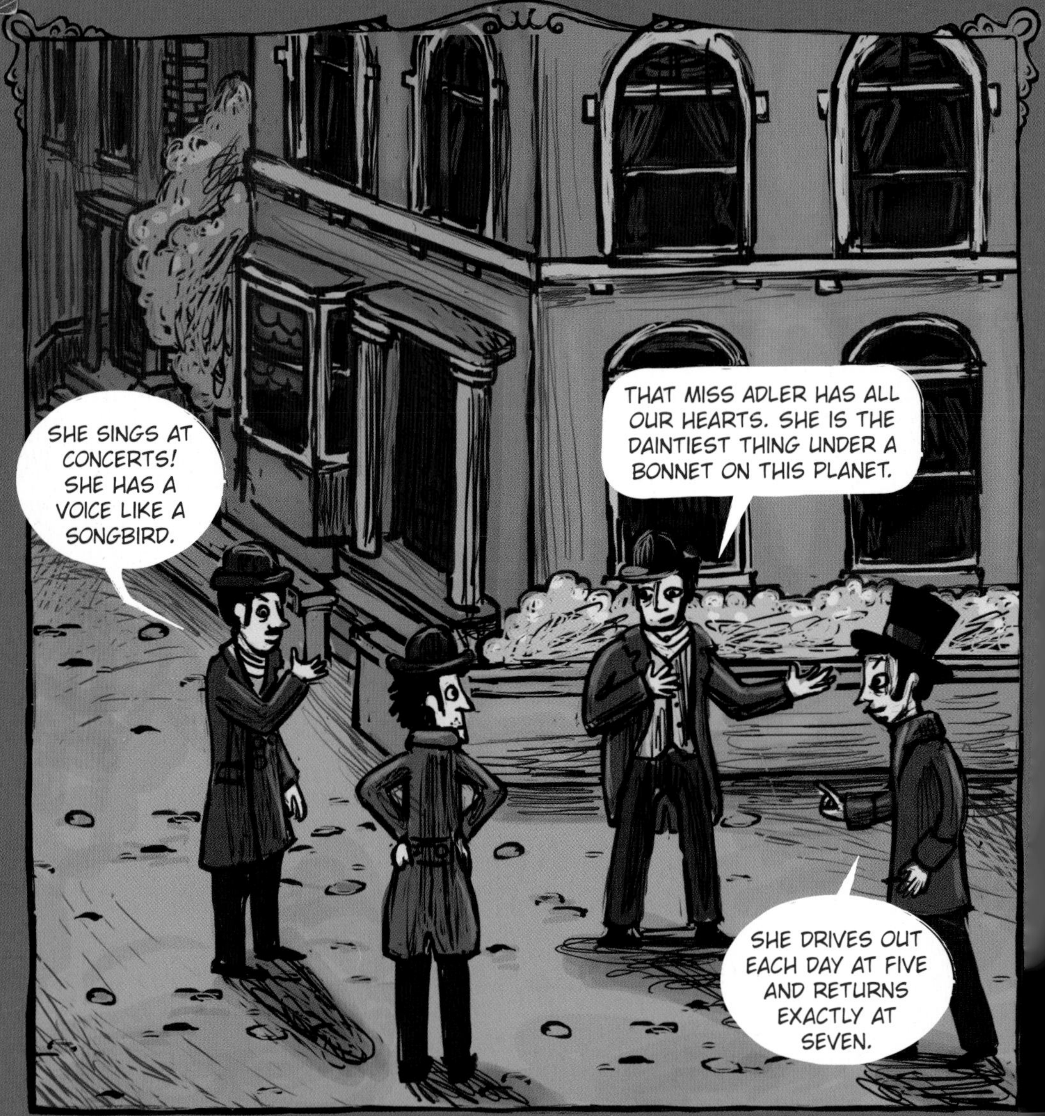
SHE SINGS AT CONCERTS! SHE HAS A VOICE LIKE A SONGBIRD.
THAT MISS ADLER HAS ALL OUR HEARTS. SHE IS THE DAINTIEST THING UNDER A BONNET ON THIS PLANET.
SHE DRIVES OUT EACH DAY AT FIVE AND RETURNS EXACTLY AT SEVEN.

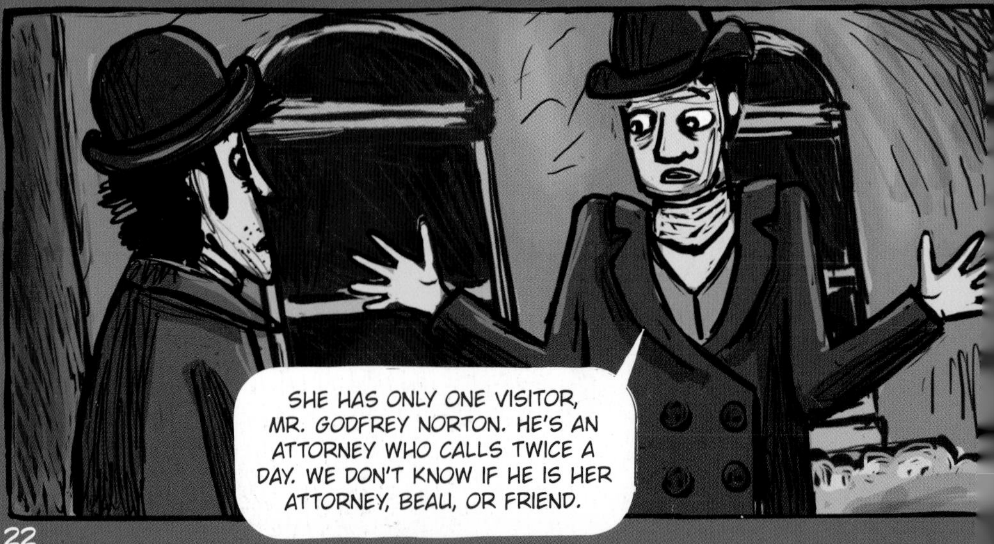
SHE HAS ONLY ONE VISITOR, MR. GODFREY NORTON. HE'S AN ATTORNEY WHO CALLS TWICE A DAY. WE DON'T KNOW IF HE IS HER ATTORNEY, BEAU, OR FRIEND.

AS I WAS FINISHING EXAMINING THE HOUSE, A HANSOM CAB PULLED UP. A MAN SIGNALED FOR THE DRIVER TO WAIT AND RUSHED INSIDE THE HOUSE.

THROUGH THE WINDOW, I WATCHED THE MAN WALK BACK AND FORTH EXCITEDLY, WAVING HIS HANDS.

SNAP!

DRIVE LIKE THE DEVIL TO THE CHURCH OF ST. MONICA ON EDGWARE ROAD. I HAVE TO BE THERE IN TWENTY MINUTES SHARP.

I WAS WONDERING WHAT I SHOULD DO JUST AS A FANCY LITTLE CARRIAGE DROVE UP. MISS ADLER SHOT OUT OF THE HOUSE.

CLIP CLOP CLIP CLOP

AS SHE STEPPED INTO THE CARRIAGE, I SAW HER FACE. IT WAS ONE A MAN MIGHT DIE FOR!

Holmes's last sentence and excited voice were certainly unexpected. Never before had his cool-headed reasoning allowed him to comment on a woman's charms. From this I deduced that Irene Adler must indeed be an exceptional lady. Holmes continued telling his story at a rapid pace . . .

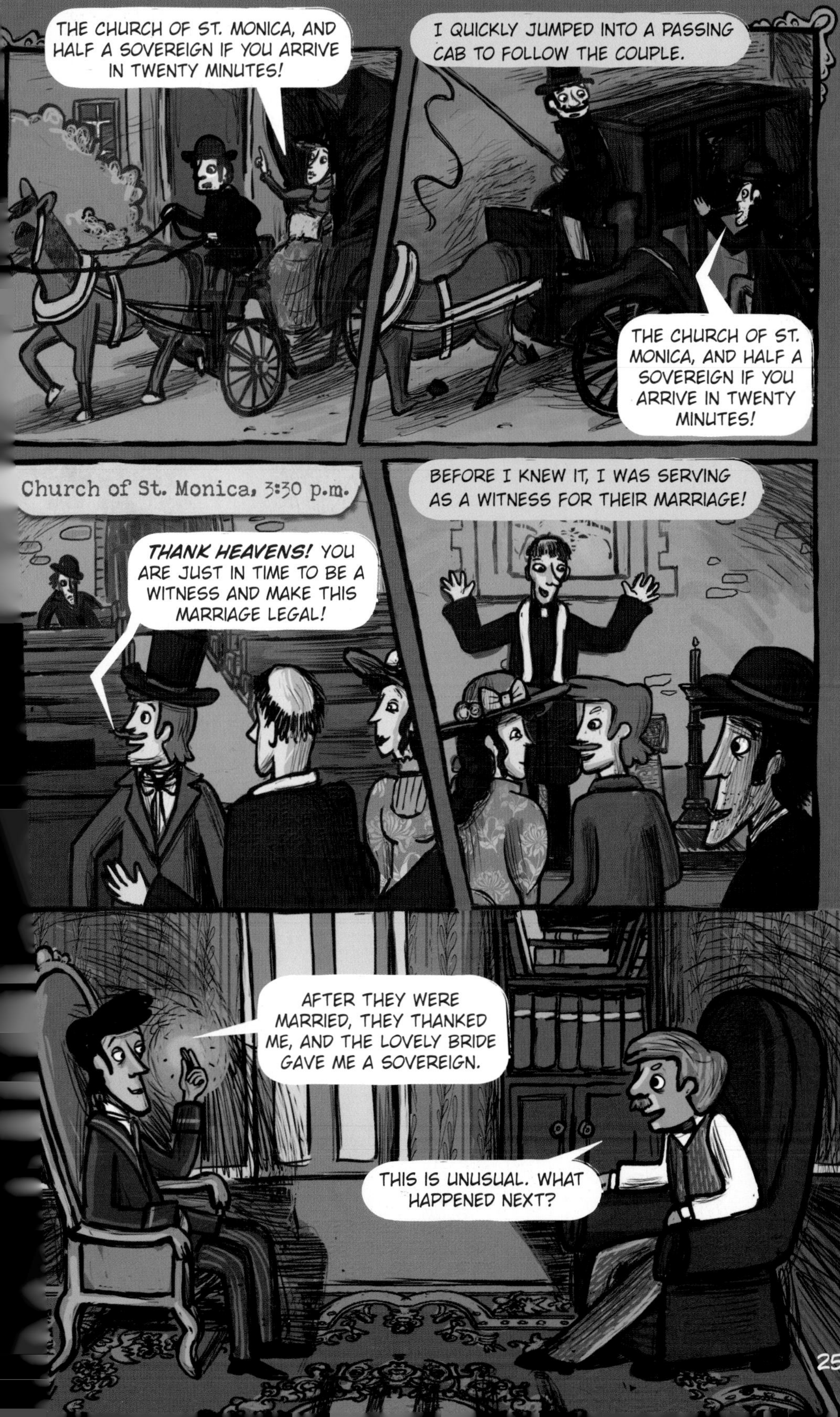
THE CHURCH OF ST. MONICA, AND HALF A SOVEREIGN IF YOU ARRIVE IN TWENTY MINUTES!
I QUICKLY JUMPED INTO A PASSING CAB TO FOLLOW THE COUPLE.
THE CHURCH OF ST. MONICA, AND HALF A SOVEREIGN IF YOU ARRIVE IN TWENTY MINUTES!
Church of St. Monica, 3:30 p.m.
THANK HEAVENS! YOU ARE JUST IN TIME TO BE A WITNESS AND MAKE THIS MARRIAGE LEGAL!
BEFORE I KNEW IT, I WAS SERVING AS A WITNESS FOR THEIR MARRIAGE!
AFTER THEY WERE MARRIED, THEY THANKED ME, AND THE LOVELY BRIDE GAVE ME A SOVEREIGN.
THIS IS UNUSUAL. WHAT HAPPENED NEXT?

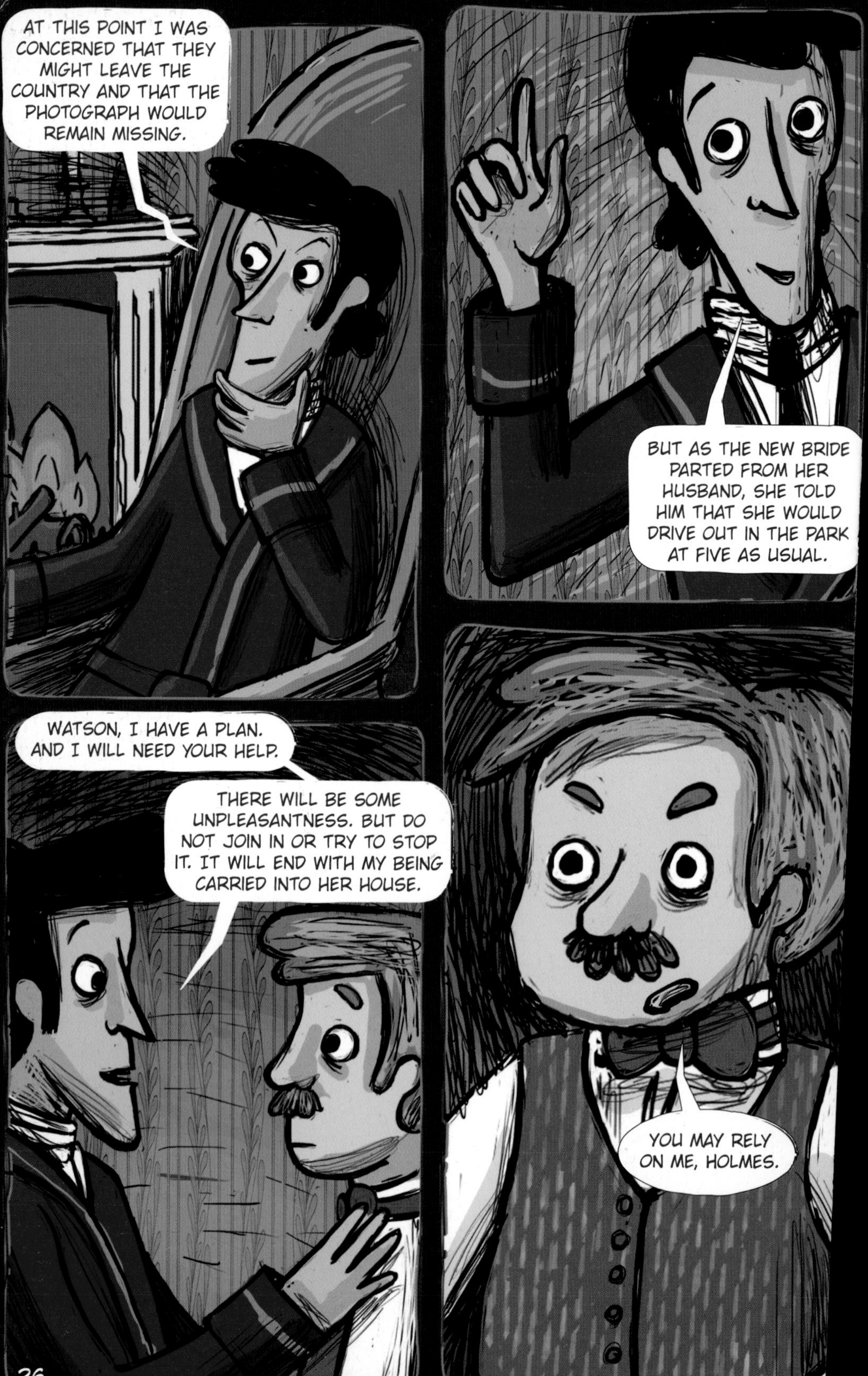

AT THIS POINT I WAS CONCERNED THAT THEY MIGHT LEAVE THE COUNTRY AND THAT THE PHOTOGRAPH WOULD REMAIN MISSING.
BUT AS THE NEW BRIDE PARTED FROM HER HUSBAND, SHE TOLD HIM THAT SHE WOULD DRIVE OUT IN THE PARK AT FIVE AS USUAL.
WATSON, I HAVE A PLAN. AND I WILL NEED YOUR HELP.
THERE WILL BE SOME UNPLEASANTNESS. BUT DO NOT JOIN IN OR TRY TO STOP IT. IT WILL END WITH MY BEING CARRIED INTO HER HOUSE.
YOU MAY RELY ON ME, HOLMES.

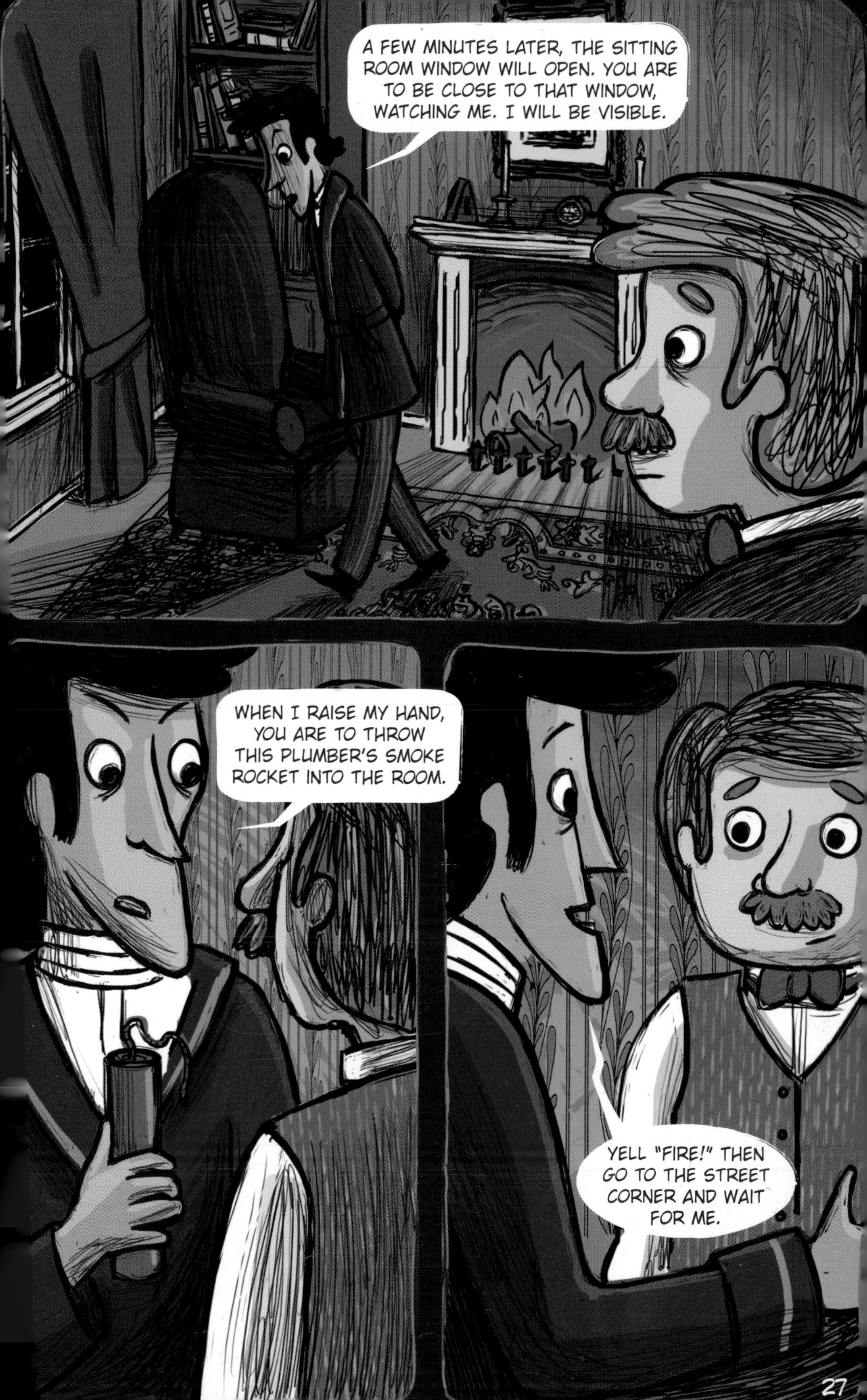
A FEW MINUTES LATER, THE SITTING ROOM WINDOW WILL OPEN. YOU ARE TO BE CLOSE TO THAT WINDOW, WATCHING ME. I WILL BE VISIBLE.
WHEN I RAISE MY HAND, YOU ARE TO THROW THIS PLUMBER'S SMOKE ROCKET INTO THE ROOM.
YELL "FIRE!" THEN GO TO THE STREET CORNER AND WAIT FOR ME.

Holmes went into his bedroom and soon returned looking like a gentle, simple-minded country clergyman. A broadcloth hat, baggy trousers, white tie, and worn black coat had transformed the Holmes I knew. He peered at me through small wire spectacles and piously folded his hands. I had to laugh. The stage had lost a fine actor when Holmes turned his talents to solving crime. It was time to make our way to the lady's house.

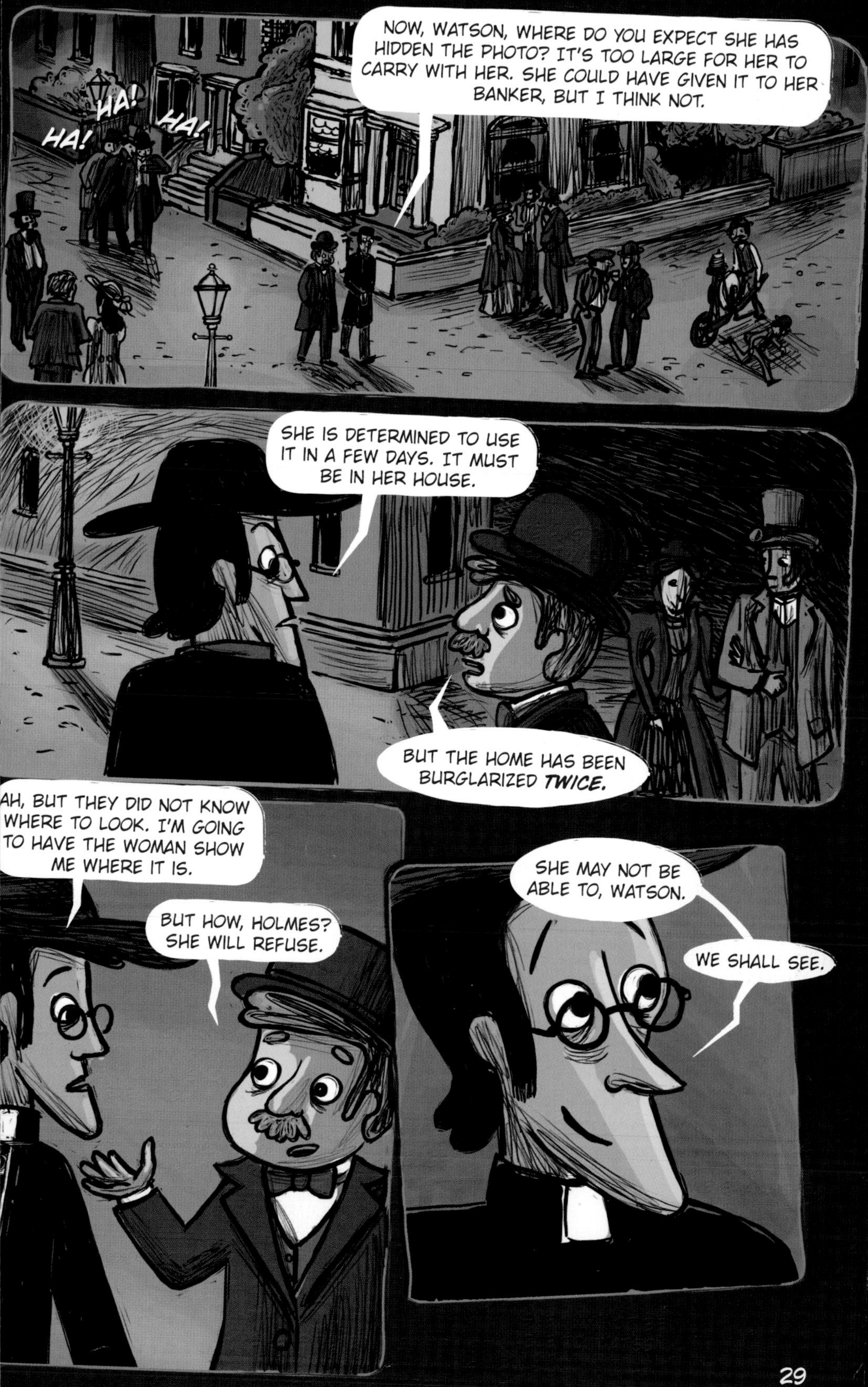
HA!
HA!
HA!
NOW, WATSON, WHERE DO YOU EXPECT SHE HAS HIDDEN THE PHOTO? IT'S TOO LARGE FOR HER TO CARRY WITH HER. SHE COULD HAVE GIVEN IT TO HER BANKER, BUT I THINK NOT.
SHE IS DETERMINED TO USE IT IN A FEW DAYS. IT MUST BE IN HER HOUSE.
BUT THE HOME HAS BEEN BURGLARIZED *TWICE.*
AH, BUT THEY DID NOT KNOW WHERE TO LOOK. I'M GOING TO HAVE THE WOMAN SHOW ME WHERE IT IS.
BUT HOW, HOLMES? SHE WILL REFUSE.
SHE MAY NOT BE ABLE TO, WATSON.
WE SHALL SEE.

Just then a carriage approached the lodge. As the carriage slowed, several guardsmen rushed to open the door for the woman inside, in hopes of earning a coin or two. I watched as one shoved another, and a fierce quarrel broke out. In an instant, the lady was in the midst of a group of angry men.

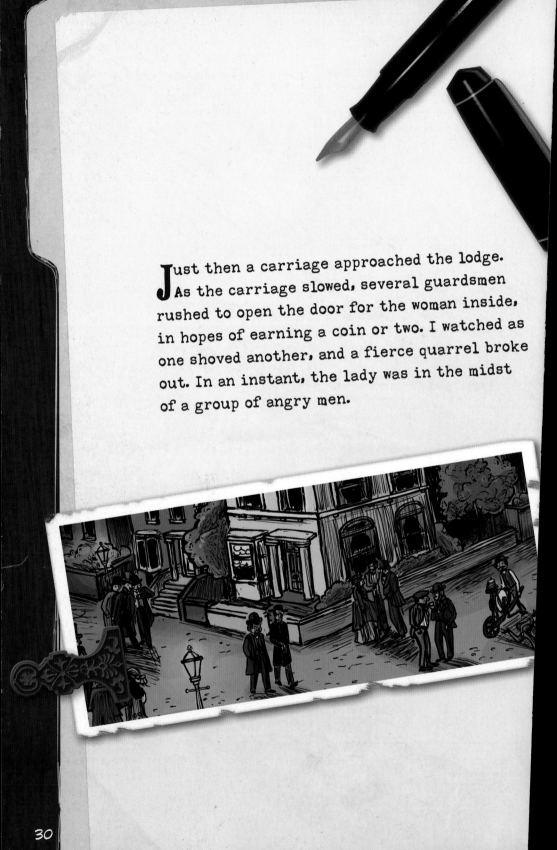

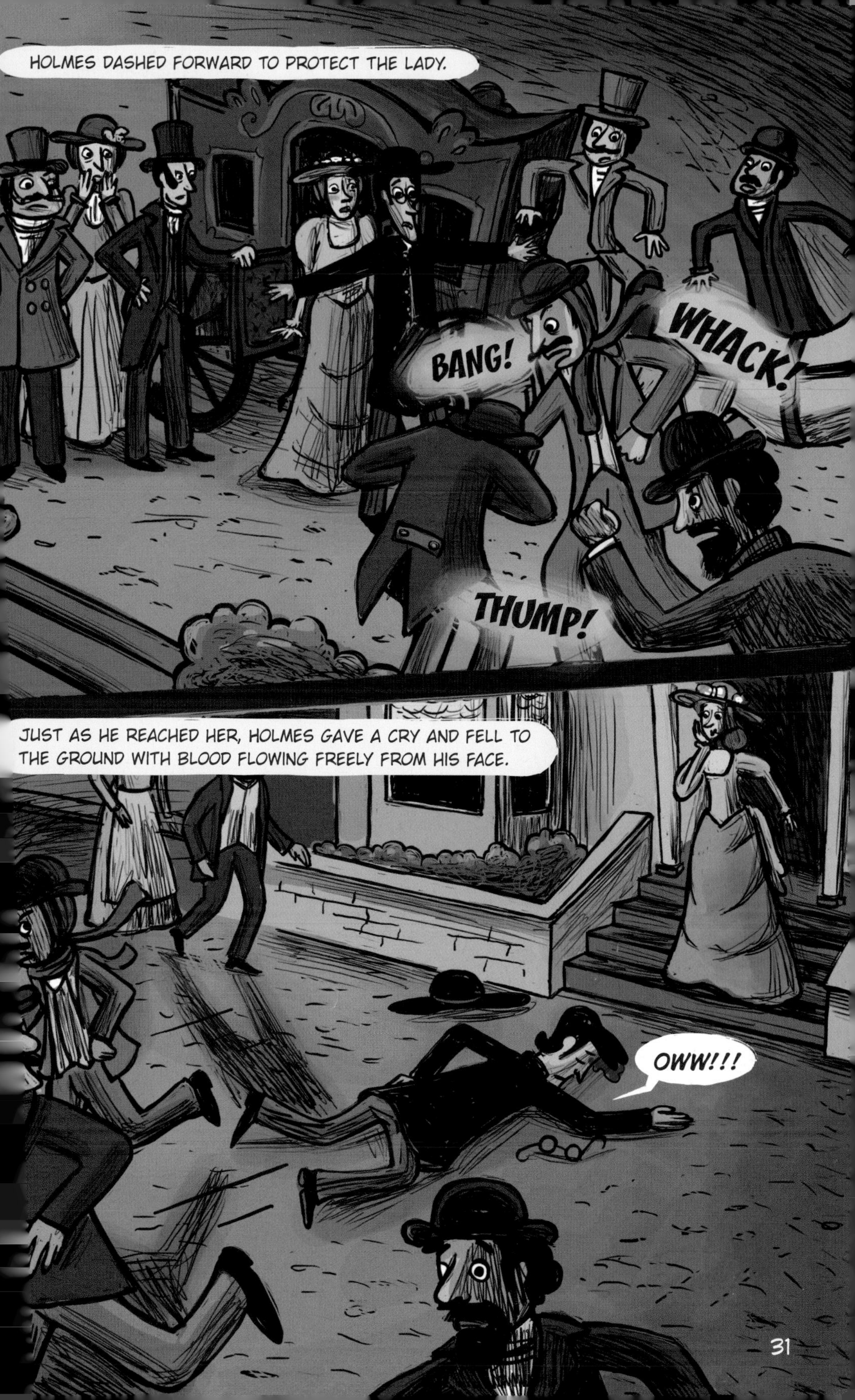
HOLMES DASHED FORWARD TO PROTECT THE LADY.
BANG!
WHACK!
THUMP!
JUST AS HE REACHED HER, HOLMES GAVE A CRY AND FELL TO THE GROUND WITH BLOOD FLOWING FREELY FROM HIS FACE.
OWW!!!

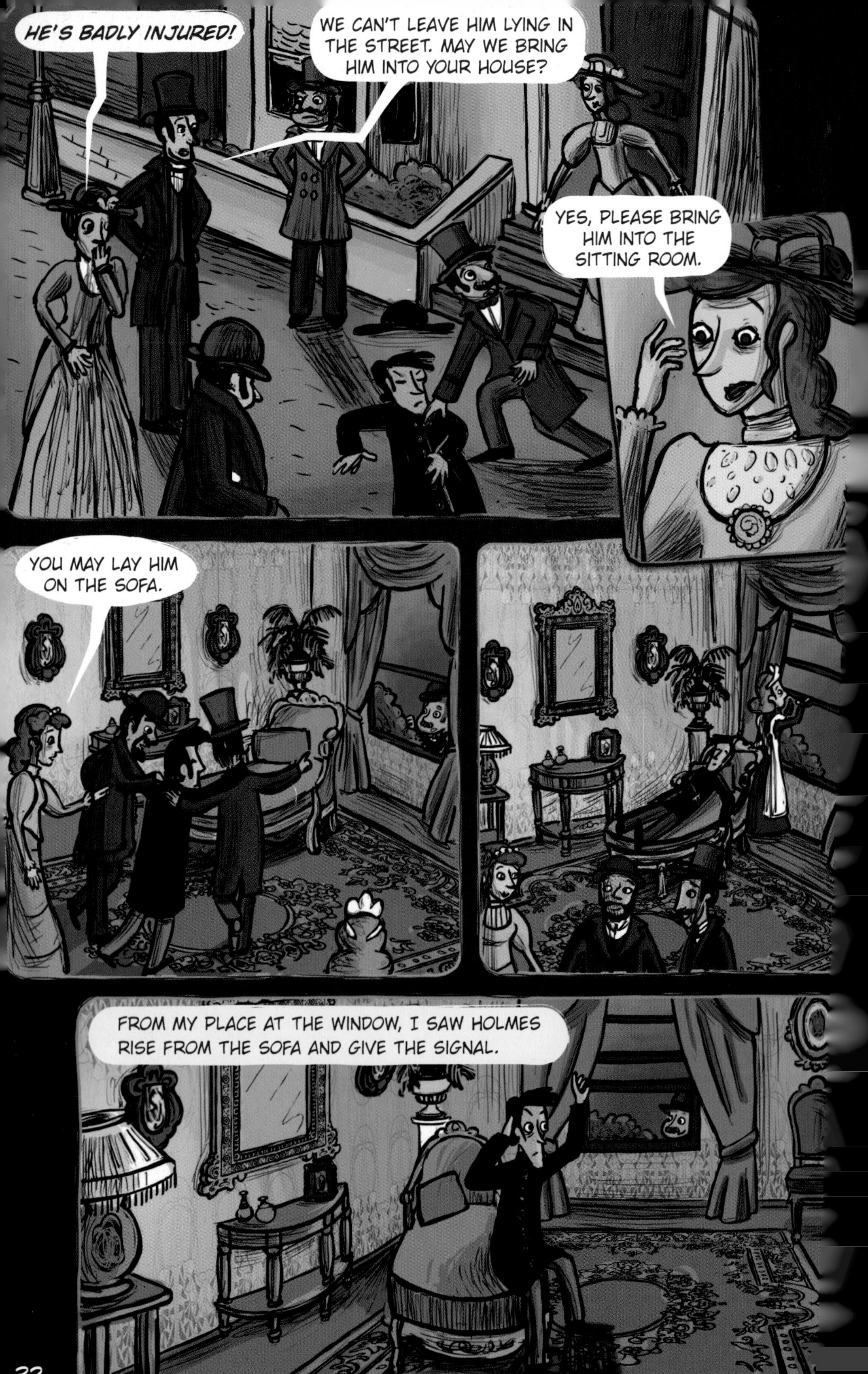
HE'S BADLY INJURED!
WE CAN'T LEAVE HIM LYING IN THE STREET. MAY WE BRING HIM INTO YOUR HOUSE?
YES, PLEASE BRING HIM INTO THE SITTING ROOM.
YOU MAY LAY HIM ON THE SOFA.
FROM MY PLACE AT THE WINDOW, I SAW HOLMES RISE FROM THE SOFA AND GIVE THE SIGNAL.

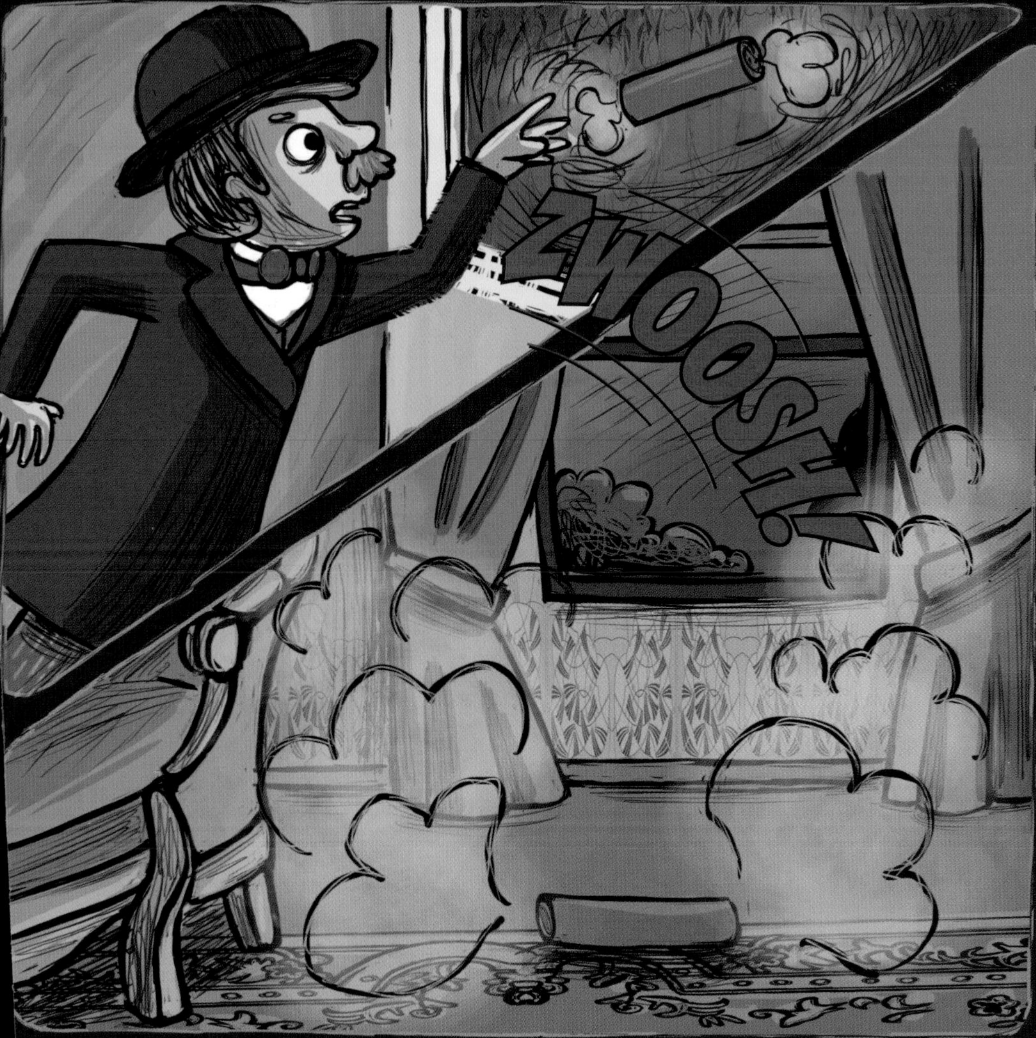
ZWOOSH!

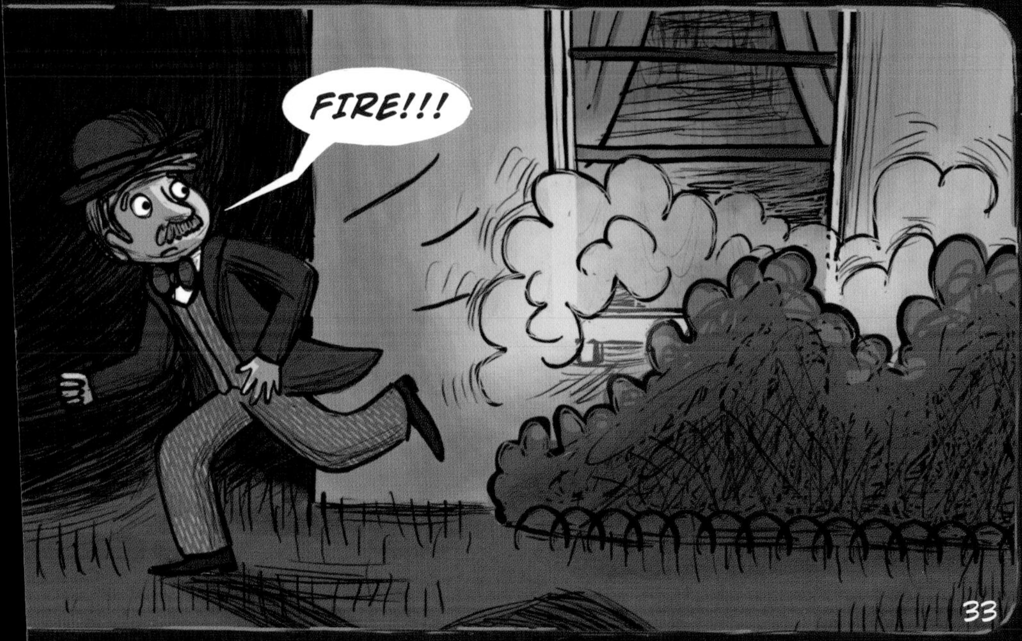
FIRE!!!

Inside, people were rushing around until the maid found the bomb and yelled out "false alarm." I slipped away to the street corner, where I was soon joined by the disguised Holmes. We walked swiftly down Serpentine Avenue without talking until we reached the quieter streets of Edgware Road. I was dying to know if he had discovered the photograph.

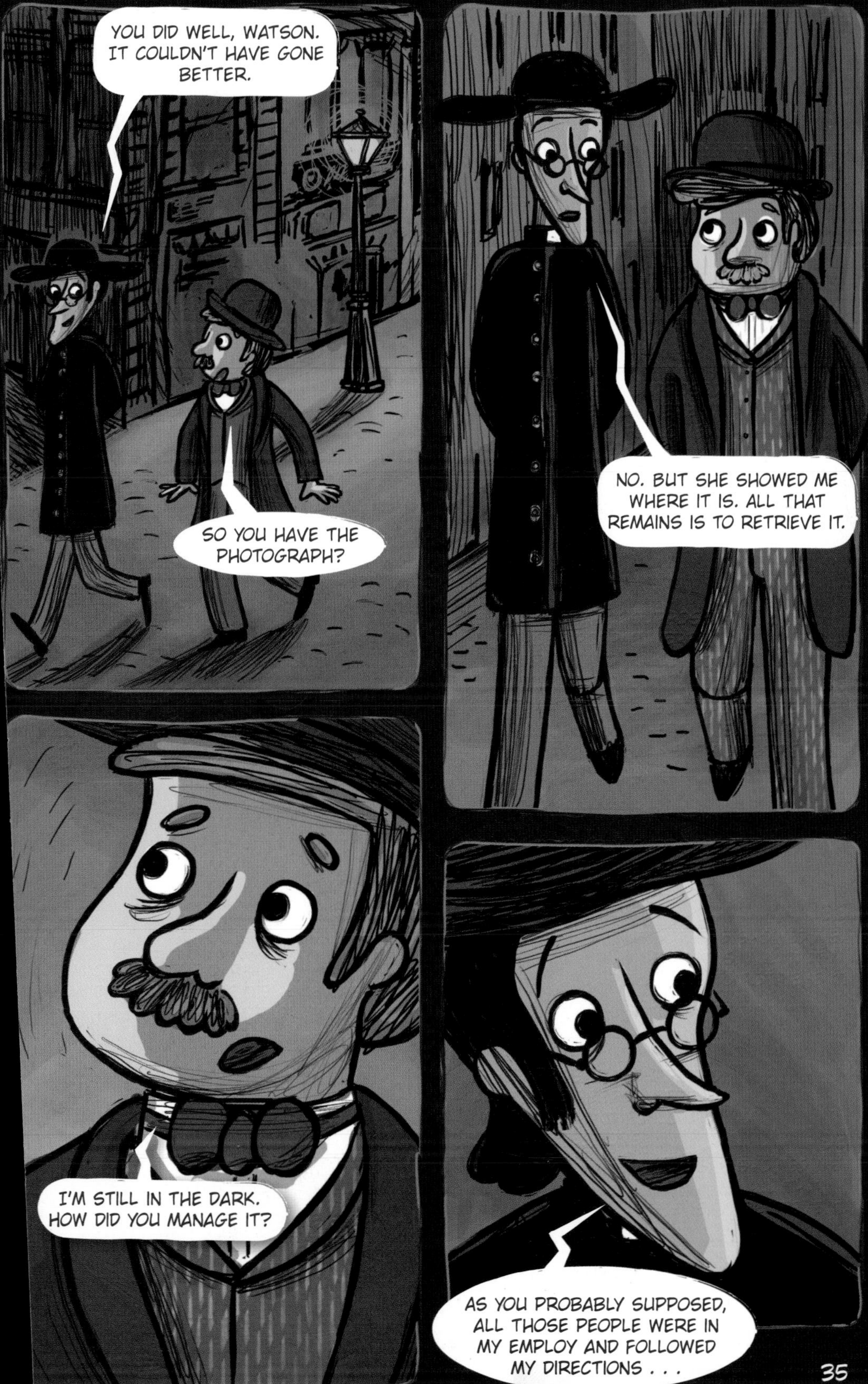
YOU DID WELL, WATSON. IT COULDN'T HAVE GONE BETTER.
SO YOU HAVE THE PHOTOGRAPH?
NO. BUT SHE SHOWED ME WHERE IT IS. ALL THAT REMAINS IS TO RETRIEVE IT.
I'M STILL IN THE DARK. HOW DID YOU MANAGE IT?
AS YOU PROBABLY SUPPOSED, ALL THOSE PEOPLE WERE IN MY EMPLOY AND FOLLOWED MY DIRECTIONS . . .

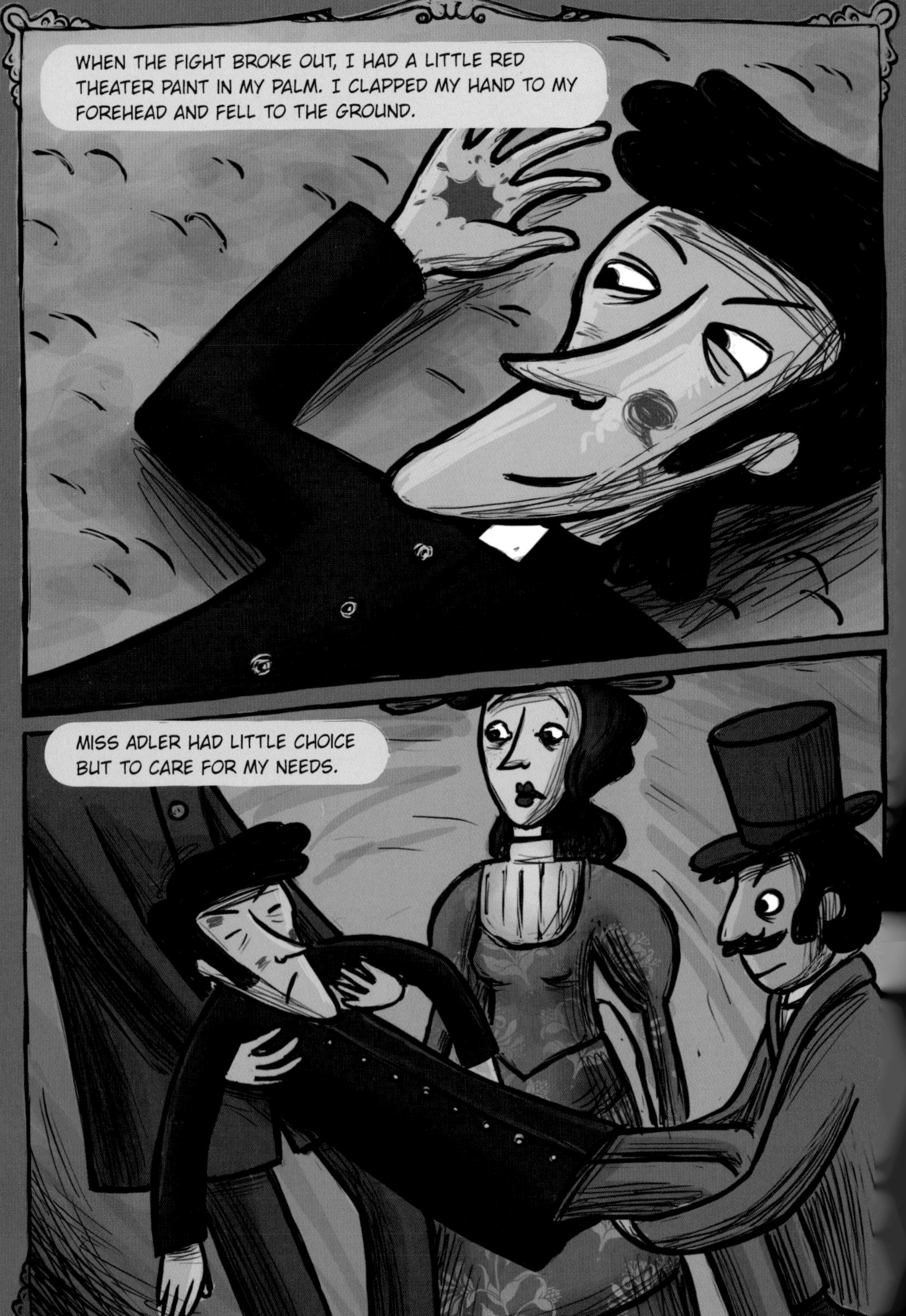
WHEN THE FIGHT BROKE OUT, I HAD A LITTLE RED THEATER PAINT IN MY PALM. I CLAPPED MY HAND TO MY FOREHEAD AND FELL TO THE GROUND.
MISS ADLER HAD LITTLE CHOICE BUT TO CARE FOR MY NEEDS.

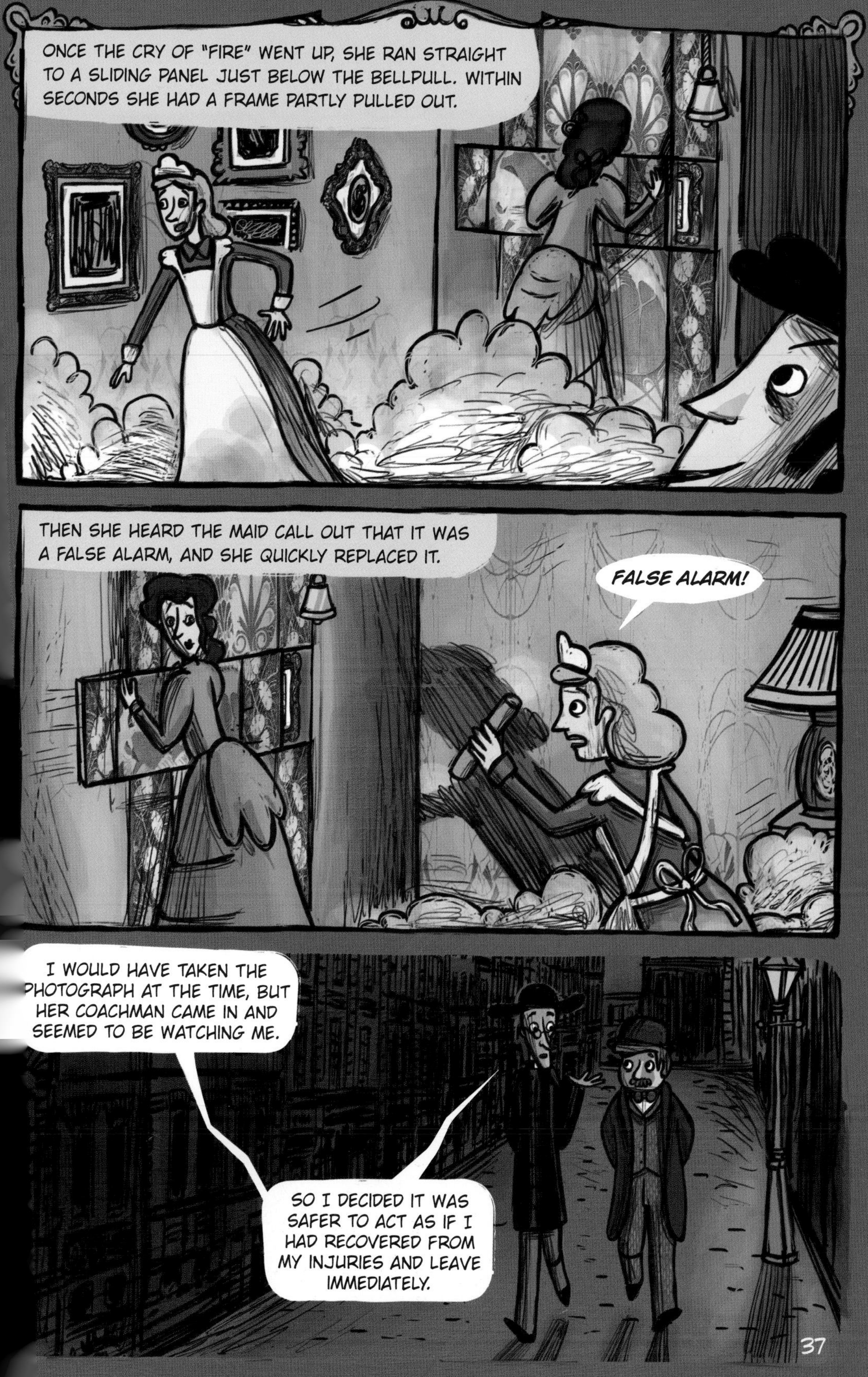
ONCE THE CRY OF "FIRE" WENT UP, SHE RAN STRAIGHT TO A SLIDING PANEL JUST BELOW THE BELLPULL. WITHIN SECONDS SHE HAD A FRAME PARTLY PULLED OUT.
THEN SHE HEARD THE MAID CALL OUT THAT IT WAS A FALSE ALARM, AND SHE QUICKLY REPLACED IT.
FALSE ALARM!
I WOULD HAVE TAKEN THE PHOTOGRAPH AT THE TIME, BUT HER COACHMAN CAME IN AND SEEMED TO BE WATCHING ME.
SO I DECIDED IT WAS SAFER TO ACT AS IF I HAD RECOVERED FROM MY INJURIES AND LEAVE IMMEDIATELY.

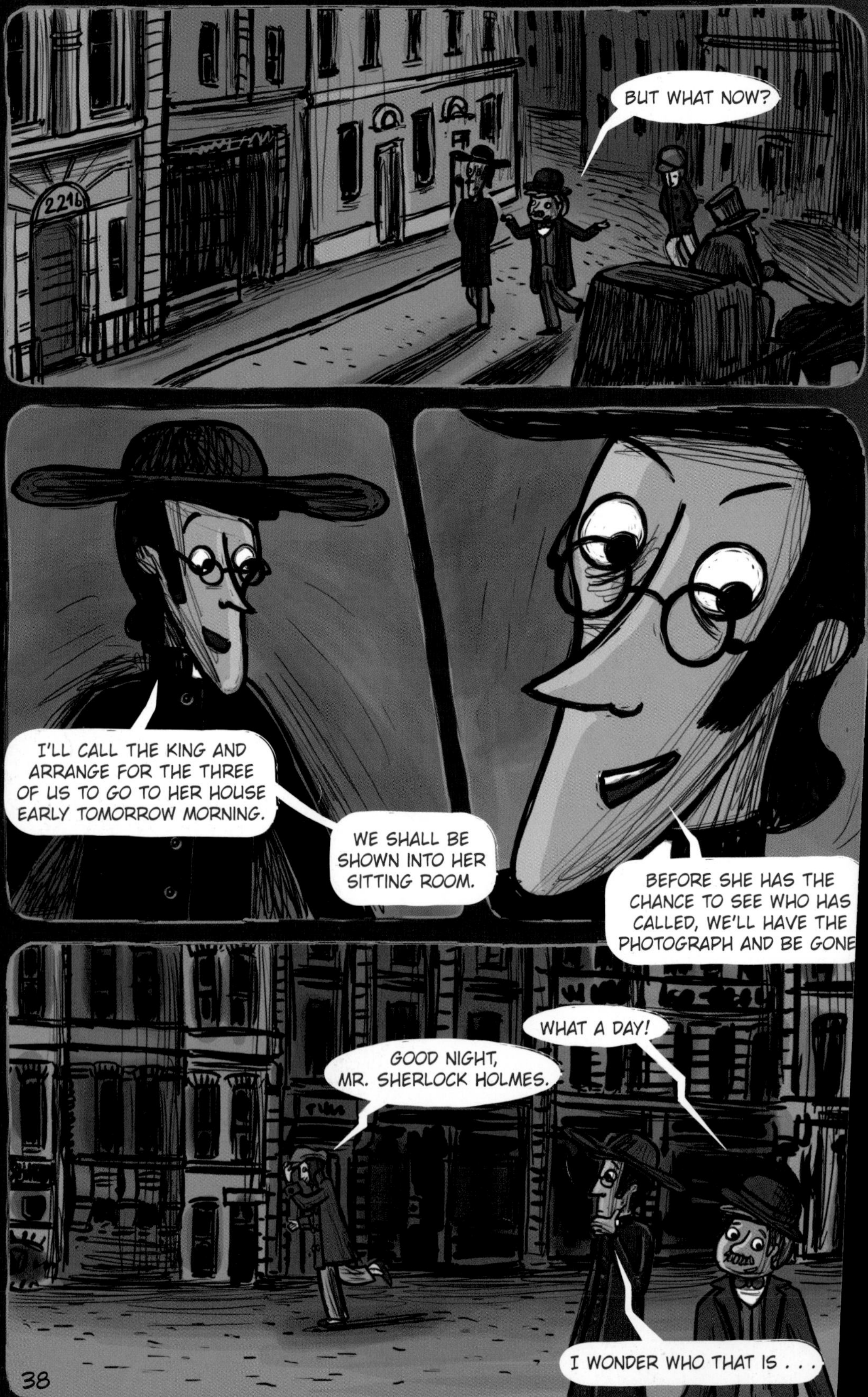
BUT WHAT NOW?
I'LL CALL THE KING AND ARRANGE FOR THE THREE OF US TO GO TO HER HOUSE EARLY TOMORROW MORNING.
WE SHALL BE SHOWN INTO HER SITTING ROOM.
BEFORE SHE HAS THE CHANCE TO SEE WHO HAS CALLED, WE'LL HAVE THE PHOTOGRAPH AND BE GONE
GOOD NIGHT, MR. SHERLOCK HOLMES.
WHAT A DAY!
I WONDER WHO THAT IS . . .

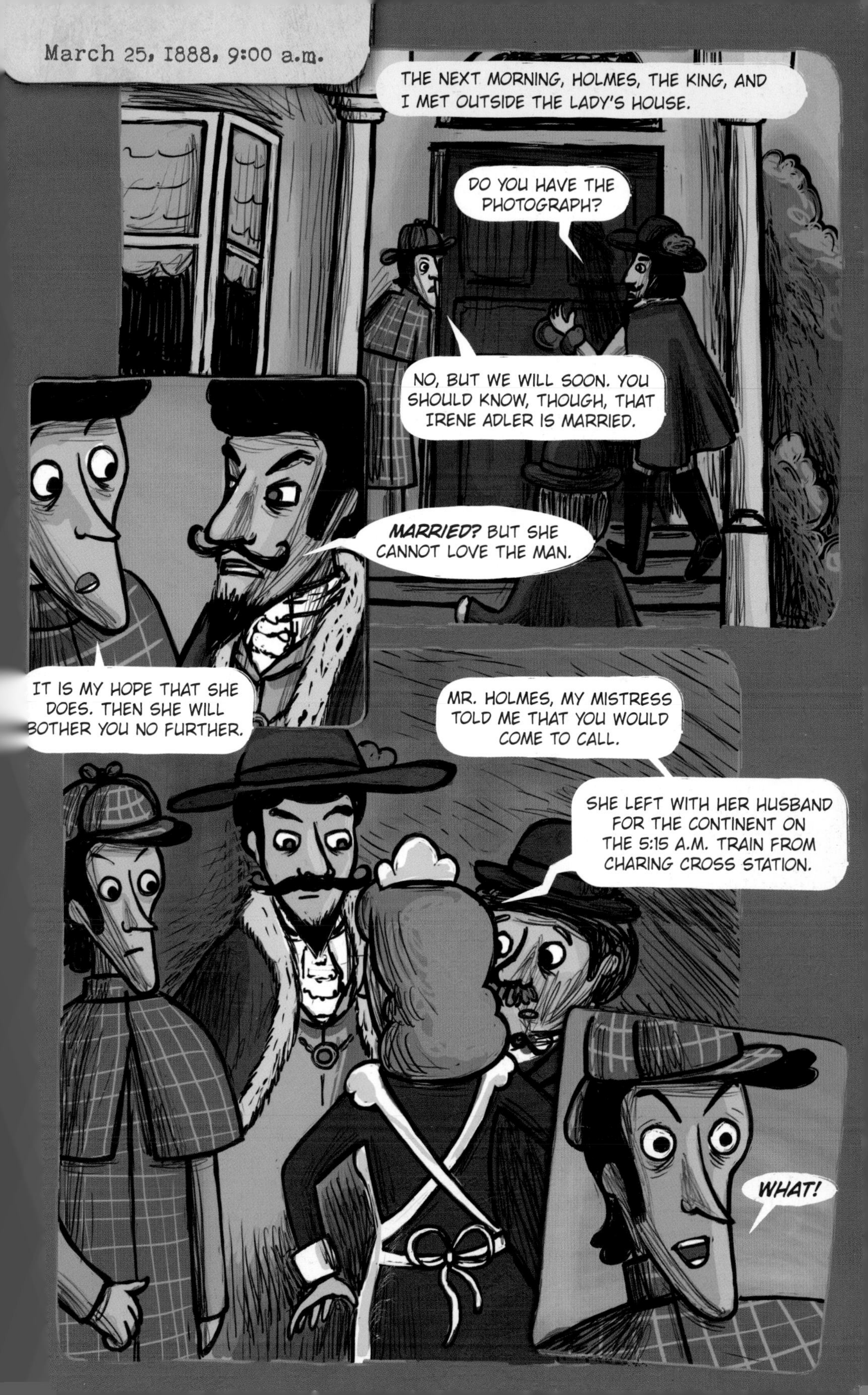
March 25, 1888, 9:00 a.m.
THE NEXT MORNING, HOLMES, THE KING, AND I MET OUTSIDE THE LADY'S HOUSE.
DO YOU HAVE THE PHOTOGRAPH?
NO, BUT WE WILL SOON. YOU SHOULD KNOW, THOUGH, THAT IRENE ADLER IS MARRIED.
MARRIED? BUT SHE CANNOT LOVE THE MAN.
IT IS MY HOPE THAT SHE DOES. THEN SHE WILL BOTHER YOU NO FURTHER.
MR. HOLMES, MY MISTRESS TOLD ME THAT YOU WOULD COME TO CALL.
SHE LEFT WITH HER HUSBAND FOR THE CONTINENT ON THE 5:15 A.M. TRAIN FROM CHARING CROSS STATION.
WHAT!

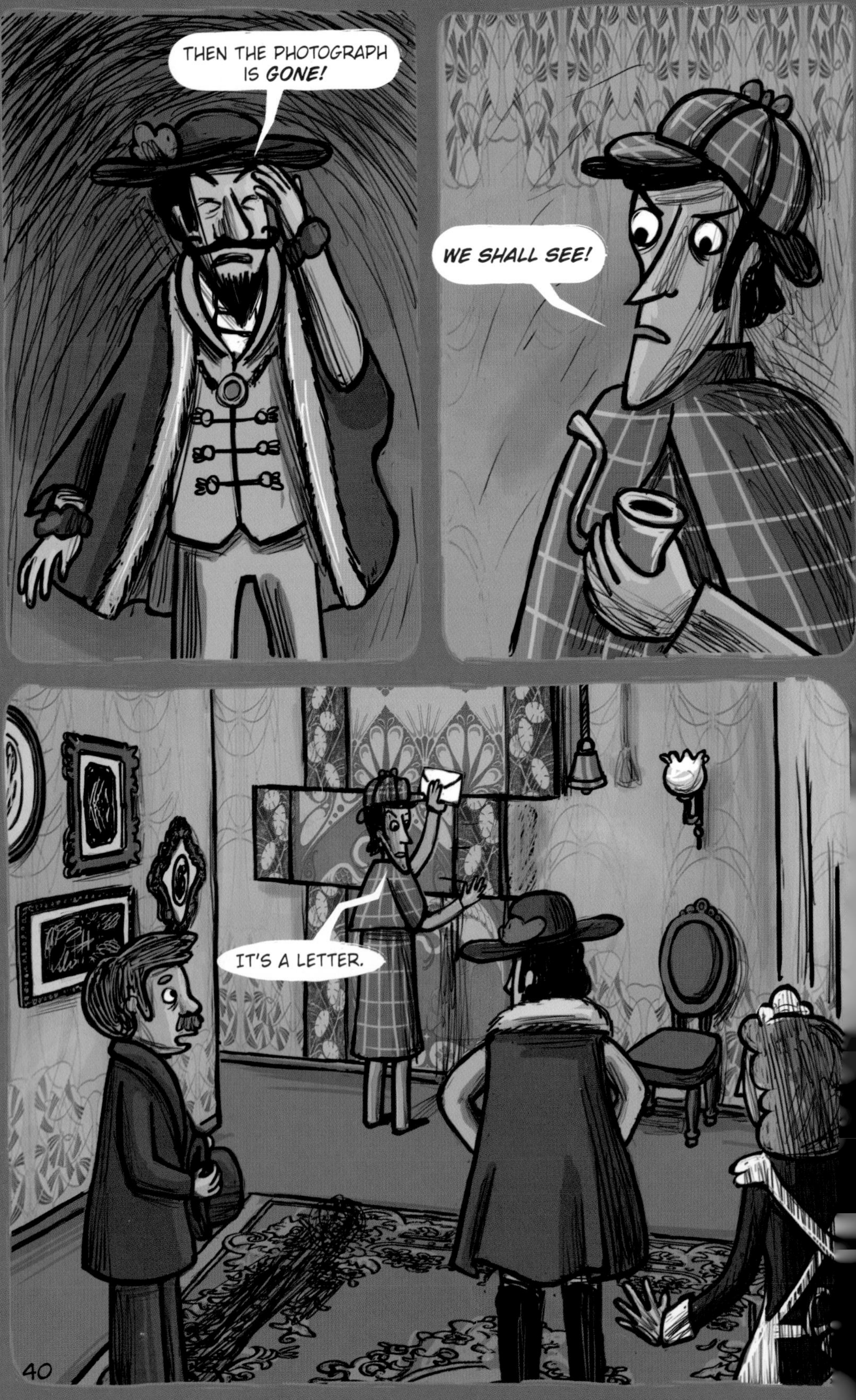
THEN THE PHOTOGRAPH IS GONE!
WE SHALL SEE!
IT'S A LETTER.

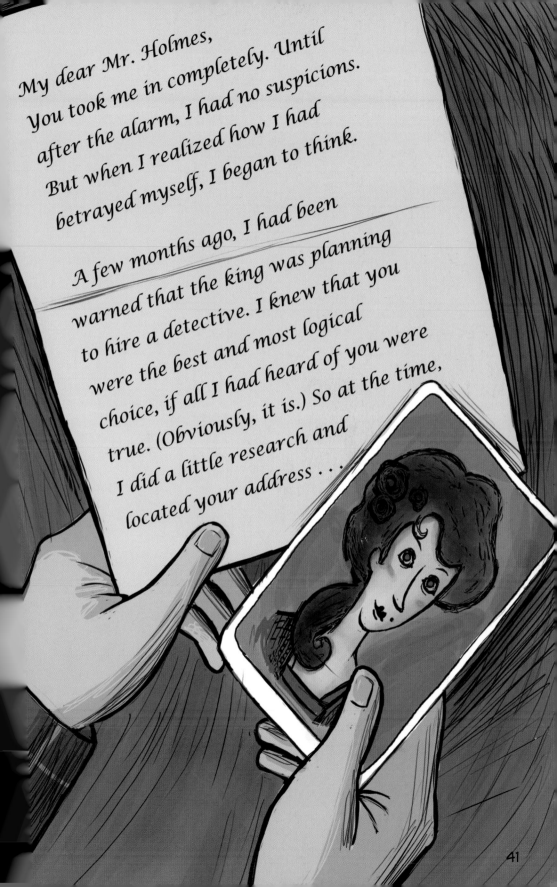

My dear Mr. Holmes,

You took me in completely. Until after the alarm, I had no suspicions. But when I realized how I had betrayed myself, I began to think.

A few months ago, I had been warned that the king was planning to hire a detective. I knew that you were the best and most logical choice, if all I had heard of you were true. (Obviously, it is.) So at the time, I did a little research and located your address . . .

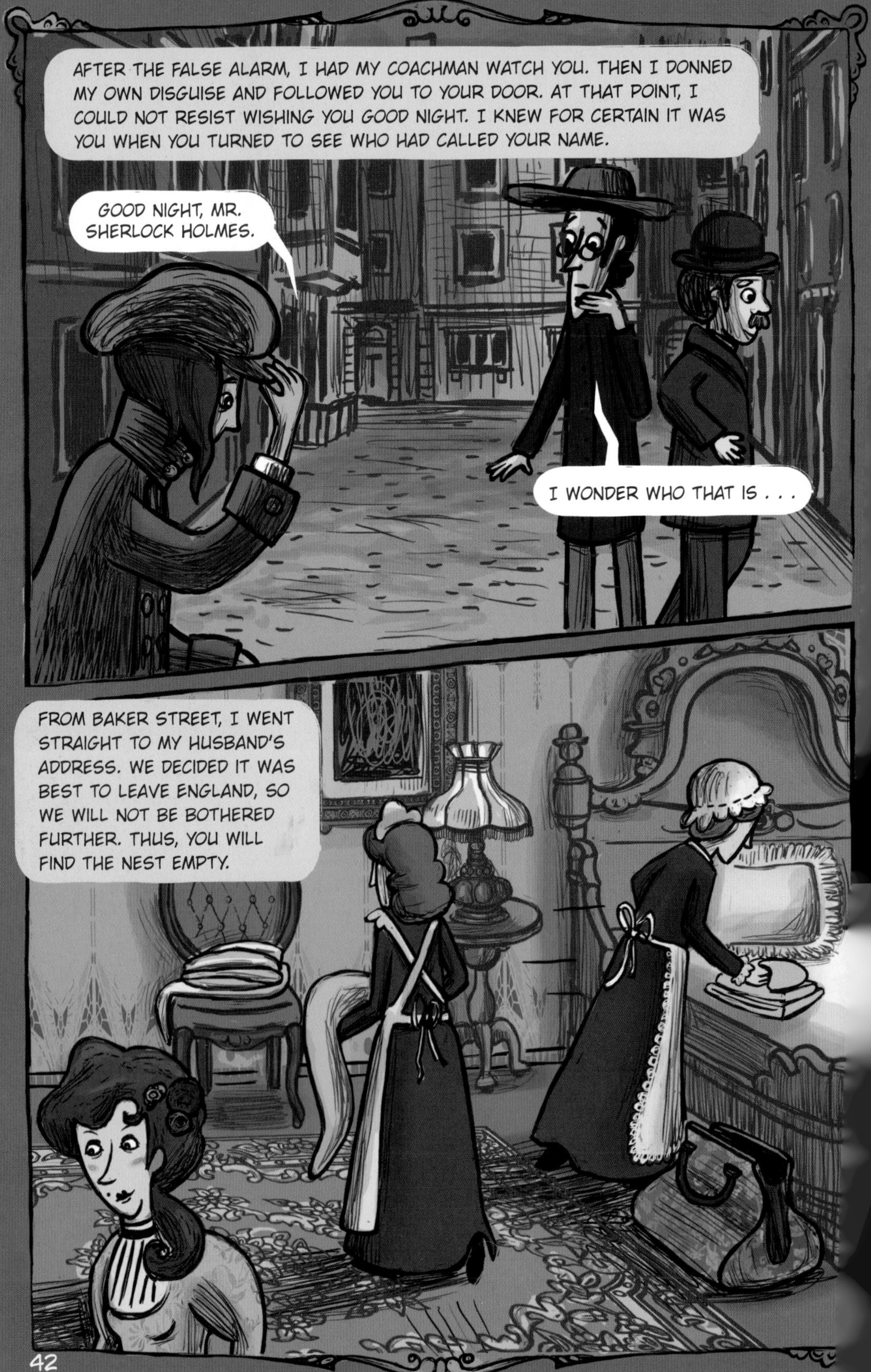
AFTER THE FALSE ALARM, I HAD MY COACHMAN WATCH YOU. THEN I DONNED MY OWN DISGUISE AND FOLLOWED YOU TO YOUR DOOR. AT THAT POINT, I COULD NOT RESIST WISHING YOU GOOD NIGHT. I KNEW FOR CERTAIN IT WAS YOU WHEN YOU TURNED TO SEE WHO HAD CALLED YOUR NAME.
GOOD NIGHT, MR. SHERLOCK HOLMES.
I WONDER WHO THAT IS . . .
FROM BAKER STREET, I WENT STRAIGHT TO MY HUSBAND'S ADDRESS. WE DECIDED IT WAS BEST TO LEAVE ENGLAND, SO WE WILL NOT BE BOTHERED FURTHER. THUS, YOU WILL FIND THE NEST EMPTY.

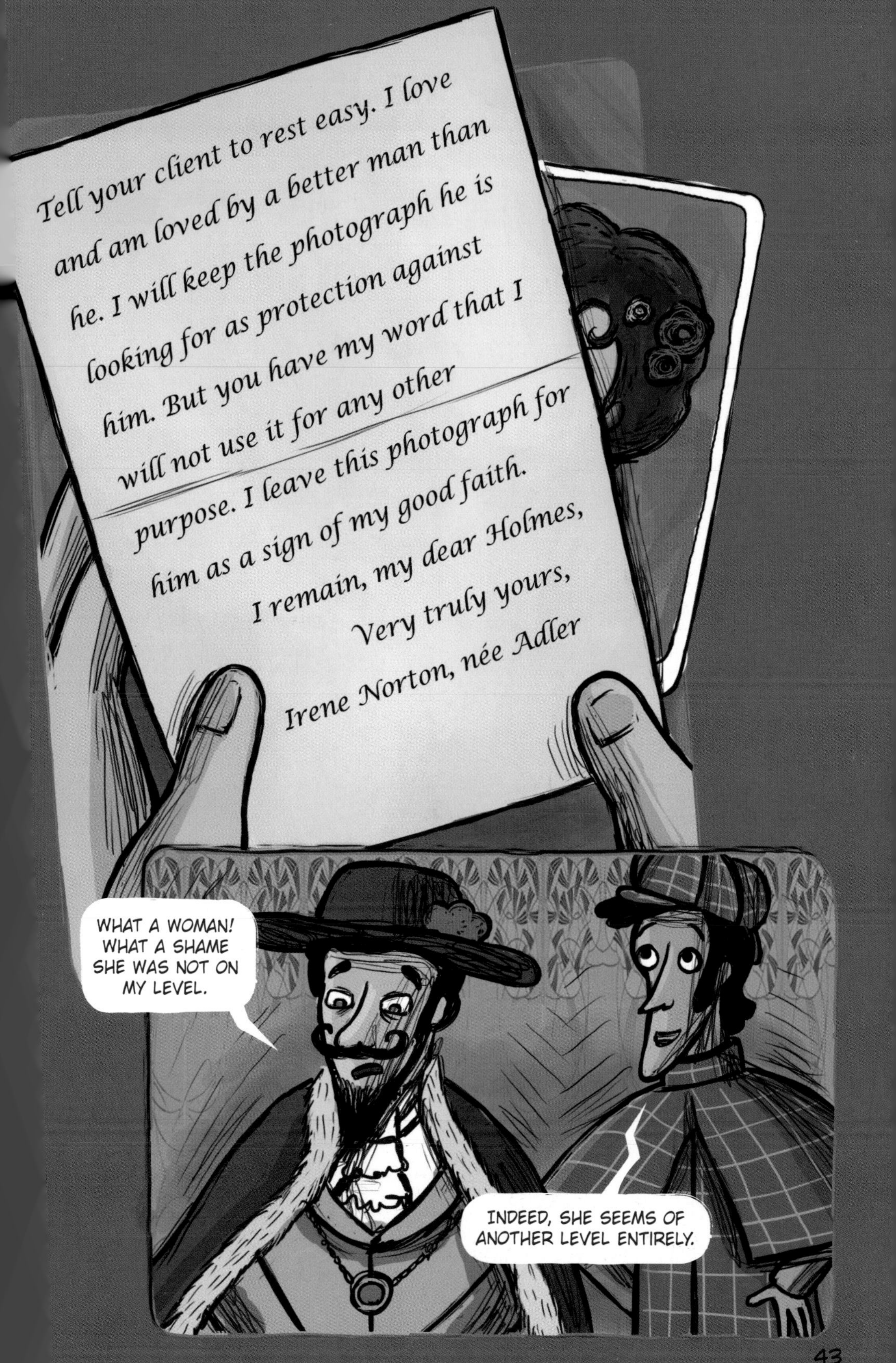
Tell your client to rest easy. I love and am loved by a better man than he. I will keep the photograph he is looking for as protection against him. But you have my word that I will not use it for any other purpose. I leave this photograph for him as a sign of my good faith.
I remain, my dear Holmes,
Very truly yours,
Irene Norton, née Adler
WHAT A WOMAN! WHAT A SHAME SHE WAS NOT ON MY LEVEL.
INDEED, SHE SEEMS OF ANOTHER LEVEL ENTIRELY.

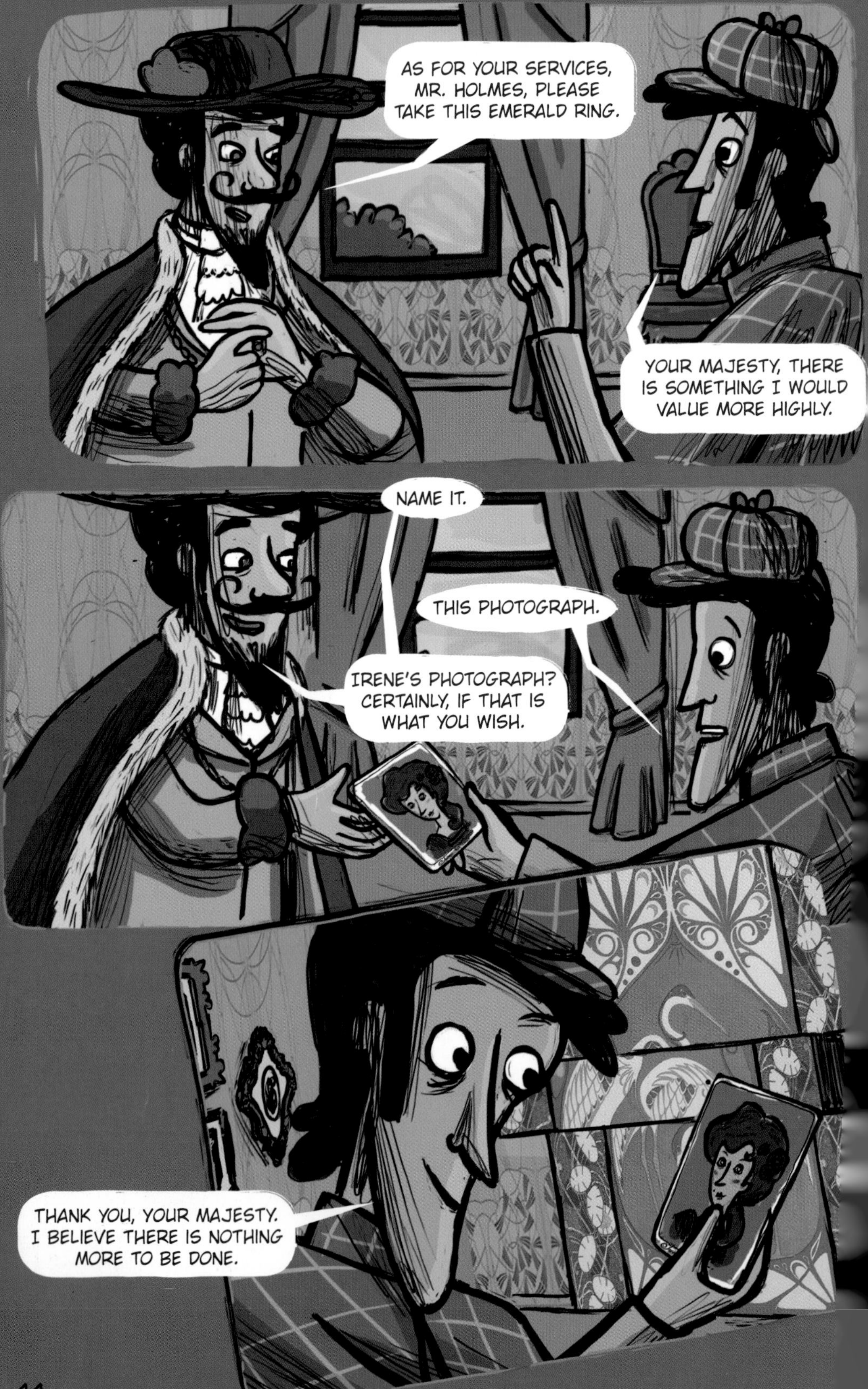
AS FOR YOUR SERVICES, MR. HOLMES, PLEASE TAKE THIS EMERALD RING.
YOUR MAJESTY, THERE IS SOMETHING I WOULD VALUE MORE HIGHLY.
NAME IT.
THIS PHOTOGRAPH.
IRENE'S PHOTOGRAPH? CERTAINLY, IF THAT IS WHAT YOU WISH.
THANK YOU, YOUR MAJESTY. I BELIEVE THERE IS NOTHING MORE TO BE DONE.

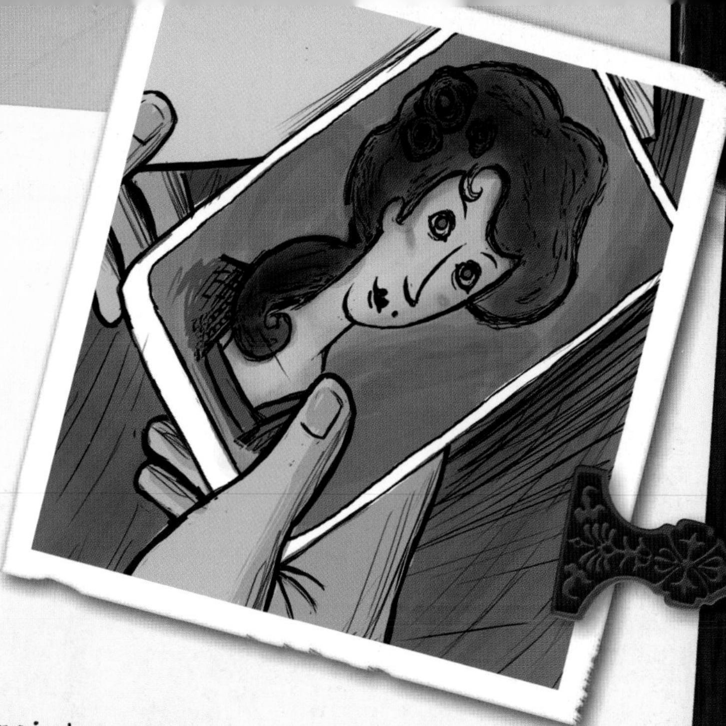

From that point on, Holmes never again referred to Irene Norton (née Adler) by her name. She has always been called, with the greatest honor—the woman. There has been no other for Holmes. She did what few could do—she outsmarted him.

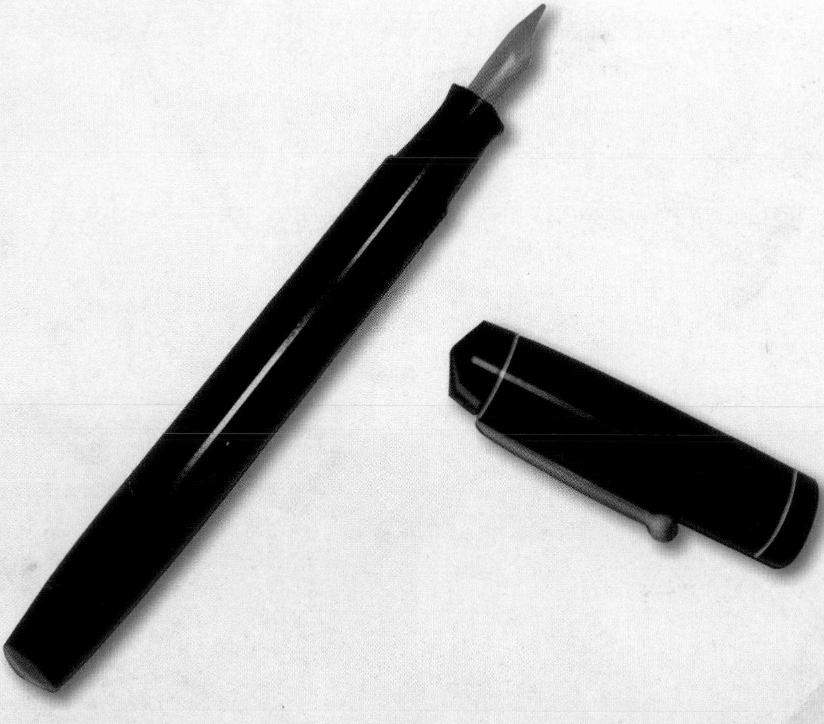

From the Desk of
John H. Watson, M.D.

A Scandal in Bohemia: How Did Holmes Solve It?

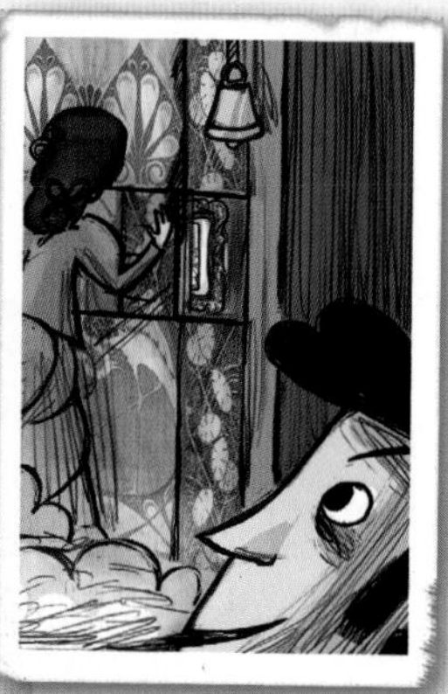

Why did Holmes suspect that Miss Adler kept the photograph in her sitting room?

From the attempts to rob her, Miss Adler knew people were looking for her photograph and letters. Holmes reasoned that she would hide them in a place where she could watch them and get a hold of them easily.

Why did Holmes stage a fight and dress as a clergyman?

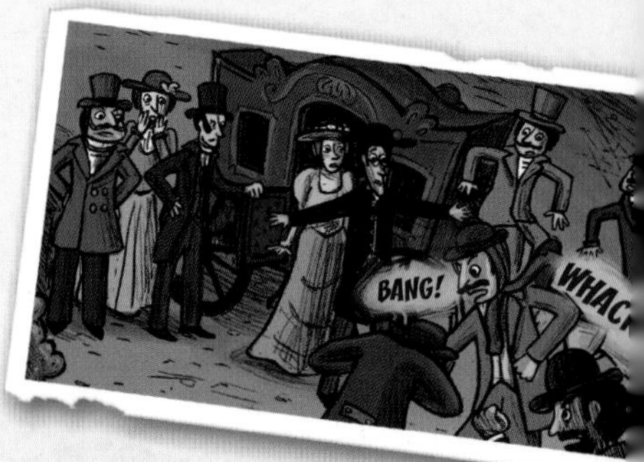
BANG!
WHAC

Miss Adler was known to be a strong-willed woman but one with a warm heart. Since burglary had failed, Holmes figured it would be better to appeal to the woman's kindness.

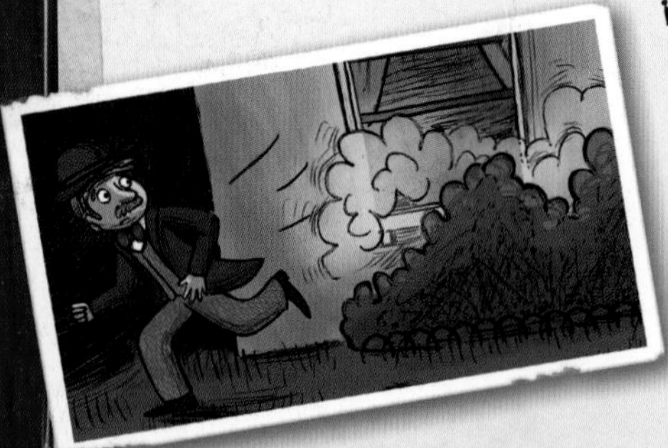

Why did Holmes fake a fire?

In the case of a fire, most people try to save their most valued possessions before fleeing the building. Holmes hoped that Miss Adler would reveal her hiding place she left.

How did Holmes fail?

Holmes underestimated his opponent's awareness and intelligence. Because of Irene Adler's great respect for Holmes's capabilities, she suspected the fake fire was the work of the master detective. She, therefore, used her acting abilities and a disguise of her own to confirm her suspicions. Thus, Miss Adler became one of the few people ever to outsmart Sherlock Holmes.

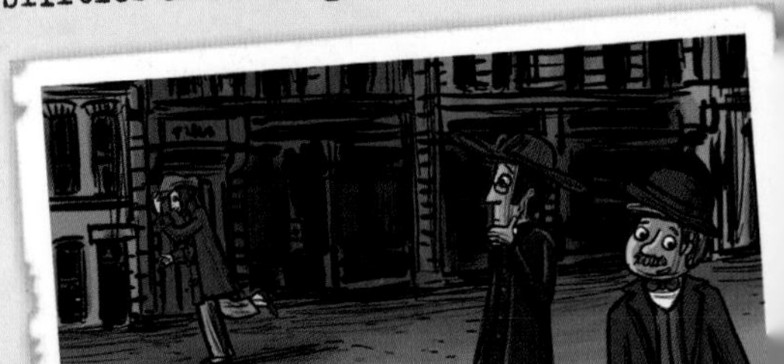

Further Reading

Gifford, Clive. *So You Think You Know London?: Over 100 Brilliant Quiz Questions.* London: Hodder & Stoughton, 2004.

Hale, Bruce. *The Chameleon Wore Chartreuse.* San Diego: Harcourt, 2000.

Horowitz, Anthony. *Stormbreaker.* New York: Philomel Books, 2001.

MysteryNet.com Sherlock Holmes
http://www.mysterynet.com/holmes

Rosellini, Eleanor. *The Puzzle in the Portrait.* Carmel: Guild Press of Indiana, 2003.

Sherlock Holmes Museum
http://www.sherlock-holmes.co.uk

Tibballs, Geoff. *Royalty's Strangest Characters: Extraordinary but True Tales from 2,000 Years of Mad Monarchs and Raving Rulers.* London: Anova Books, 2005.

221 Baker Street
http://221bakerstreet.org

Victoriana: The 19th Century Online
http://www.victoriana.com

Wilkes, Angela. *Dazzling Disguises and Clever Costumes.* New York: DK Children, 2006.

About the Author

Sir Arthur Conan Doyle was born on May 22, 1859. He became a doctor in 1882. When this career did not prove successful, Doyle started writing stories. In addition to the popular Sherlock Holmes short stories and novels, Doyle also wrote historical novels, romances, and plays.

About the Adapters

Murray Shaw's lifelong passion for Sherlock Holmes began when he was a child. He was the author of the Match Wits with Sherlock Holmes series published in the 1990s. For decades, he was a popular speaker in public schools and libraries on the adventures of Holmes and Watson.

M. J. Cosson is the author of more than fifty books, both fiction and nonfiction, for children and young adults. She has long been a fan of mysteries and especially of the great detective, Sherlock Holmes. In fact, she has participated in the production of several Sherlock Holmes plays. A native of Iowa, Cosson lives in the Texas Hill Country with her husband, dogs, and cat.

About the Illustrator

French artist Sophie Rohrbach began her career after graduating in display design at the Chambre des Commerce. She went on to design displays in many top department stores including Galeries Lafayette. She also studied illustration at Emile Cohl school in Lyon, France, where she now lives with her daughter. Rohrbach has illustrated many children's books. She is passionate about the colors and patterns that she uses in her illustrations.